W9-BBT-271

WITHDRAWN

A
Good
Journey

SIMON J. ORTIZ

811.54
O779

30, 216

Turtle Island
BERKELEY
1977

A GOOD JOURNEY. Copyright © 1977 by Simon J. Ortiz and the
Netzahaulcoyotl Historical Society.

Grateful acknowledgement is made to the following publications in
which some of the poems and narratives in this collection have ap-
peared: *Alcheringa, New Mexico Magazine, Quetzal-Vihio, America:
A Prophecy, Carriers of the Dream Wheel, The American Indian
Speaks, The Way, The Indian Rio Grande, Americans Before Colum-
bus, Treaty Council News, Zephryrus Image, Naked In The Wind.*

ISBN 0-913666-20-3
LCCN 77-82789

Thanks to the Literature Panel of the National Endowment of the
Arts for the support given towards the publication of *A Good Journey.*

A Good Journey is published by Turtle Island for the Netzahaulcoyotl
Historical Society, a non-profit corporation engaged in the multi-
cultural study of New World literature and history. For information,
address Netzahaulcoyotl Historical Society, 2845 Buena Vista Way,
Berkeley, CA 94708.

The artwork is by AARON YAVA.

Table of Contents:

Preface

TELLING

NOTES FOR MY CHILD

HOW MUCH HE REMEMBERED

Woman, This Indian Woman
Watching Salmon Jump
Some Indians At A Party
Places We Have Been
   Vada's in Cuba, New Mexico
   Northern Maine
   Indianhead Bay
   Ithaca, New York
   Upstate
   How Much Coyote Remembered
Morning By a Lakeside in Marion County, S.C.
Woman Dreamer: Slender Oak Woman
Apache Love
Her Story About Saving Herself
Two Coyote Ones

WILL COME FORTH IN TONGUES AND FURY

A Designated National Park
Long House Valley Poem
Blessings
Irish Poets on Saturday and an Indian
Ten O'clock News in the American Midwest
Grants to Gallup, New Mexico
The Following Words
"And The Land Is Just As Dry"
Vision Shadows
Heyaashi Guutah
Time to Kill in Gallup
For Our Brothers: Blue Jay, Gold Finch, Flicker, Squirrel
"The State's claim . . ."

I TELL YOU NOW

PREFACE

From an interview:

Why do you write? Who do you write for?

Because Indians always tell a story. The only way to continue is to tell a story and that's what Coyote says. The only way to continue is to tell a story and there is no other way. Your children will not survive unless you tell something about them—how they were born, how they came to this certain place, how they continued.

Who do you write for besides yourself?

For my children, for my wife, for my mother and my father and my grandparents and then reverse order that way so that I may have a good journey on my way back home.

A Good Journey

For my children,
Raho Nez and Rainy Dawn:

The stories and poems come forth
and I am only the voice telling them.
They are the true source themselves.
The words are the vision
by which we see out and in and around.

1

Telling

Telling About Coyote

Old Coyote . . .
"If he hadn't looked back
everything would have been okay
. . . like he wasn't supposed to,
               but he did,
and as soon as he did, he lost all his power,
his strength."

". . . you know, Coyote
is in the origin and all the way
through . . . he's the cause
of the trouble, the hard times
that things have . . ."

"Yet, he came so close
to having it easy.
            But he said,
"Things are just too easy . . ."
Of course he was mainly bragging,
shooting his mouth.
The existential Man,
Doestoevsky Coyote.

"He was on his way to Zuni
to get married on that Saturday,
and on the way there
he ran across a gambling party.
A number of other animals were there.
            He sat in
for a while, you know, pretty sure
of himself, you know like he is,
sure that he would win something.

                              But he lost
everything. Everything.
And that included his skin, his fur
which was the subject of envy
of all the other animals around.

Coyote had the prettiest,
the glossiest, the softest fur
that ever was. And he lost that.

            So some mice
finding him shivering in the cold
beside a rock felt sorry for him.
'This poor thing, beloved,'
they said, and they got together
just some old scraps of fur
and glued them on Coyote with pinon pitch.

And he's had that motley fur ever since.
You know, the one that looks like
scraps of an old coat, that one."

Coyote, old man, wanderer,
where you going, man?
Look up and see the sun.
Scorned, an old raggy blanket
at the back of the closet nobody wants.

"At this one conference
of all the animals there was a bird
with the purest white feathers.
His feathers were like, ah . . .
like the sun was shining on it
all the time but you could look at it
and you wouldn't be hurt by the glare.
It was easy and gentle to look at.
And he was Crow.
He was sitting at one side of the fire.
And the fire was being fed large pine logs,
and Crow was sitting downwind

from the fire, and the wind was blowing
that way . . .
            And Coyote was there.
He was envious of Crow because
all the other animals were saying,
'Wowee, look at that Crow, man,
just look at him,' admiring Crow.
Coyote began to scheme.
He kept on throwing pine logs into the fire,
ones with lots of pitch in them.
And the wind kept blowing,
all night long . . .
            Let's see,
the conference was about deciding
the seasons—when they should take place—
and it took a long time to decide that . . .
And when it was over, Crow was covered
entirely with soot. The blackest soot
from the pine logs.
And he's been like that since then."

"Oh yes, that was the conference
when Winter was decided
that it should take place
when Dog's hair got long.
            Dog said,
'I think Winter should take place
when my hair gets long.'
And it was agreed that it would. I guess
no one else offered a better reason."

            Who?
            Coyote?
O,
O yes, last time . . .
when was it,
I saw him somewhere
between Muskogee and Tulsa,
heading for Tulsy Town I guess,
just trucking along.

He was heading into some oakbrush thicket,
just over the hill was a creek.
Probably get to Tulsa in a couple days,
drink a little wine,
tease with the Pawnee babes,
sleep beside the Arkansas River,
listen to the river move,
. . . hope it don't rain,
hope the river don't rise.
He'll be back. Don't worry.
He'll be back.

They Come Around, The Wolves—
And Coyote and Crow, Too

I told you about those Wolves.
You must talk with them,
meeting them someplace,
mountain trail, desert,
at your campfire,
and call them Uncle or Brother
but never Cousin or In-law.

"I am happy that you recognized us
 and called us by the proper term,"
the Uncle said.
He was sitting there
with his hands held together,
met my eyes and then, being humble,
dropped his gaze to his hands.

"We come around
but we have a bad reputation,"
the Uncle said.
"I'm glad you came," I said.
He smiled but his eyes were sad.

"I was so pretty
and everyone like me.
My voice especially.
Everyone would stop to listen,"
said Crow.

Coyote was silent.

"I would sing and sing.
Mocking Bird and even Parrot
were jealous of me.

My feathers would shine and shine,"
said Crow.

Coyote was silent.

Thinking Coyote wasn't listening,
Crow asked, "Are you sleeping?"

"No," Coyote said.

"Did you hear what I just said?"
asked Crow.

"Yes," said Coyote.

And Crow waited for Coyote's comment.
When it didn't come, he decided to sing.

"Cawr, cawr, cawr," Crow sang.

"Stop," said Coyote.

Crow waited for the favorable comment.
He closed his eyes and made ready to bow.

Coyote silently crept away.

"Are you my friend?" asked Coyote.
"One can't be too choosey," said Crow.

Hesperus Camp, July 13, Indian 1971

Marge and Susan came up last night.
"Hello."
Faces beyond the edge of dim firelight.
"Hi. Who's that?"
"Me."
"Simon, how are you?"
"Okay."

Went to get more wood.
Fire glowed up again.
Was going to go to bed,
but I was glad they came.

Susan is from Massachusetts.
"What do you think about the Southwest?"
"Well," she said, "I wouldn't
want to live here."

You really can't tell anyone
about beauty.
They just have to see for themselves.

We made small talk.

"Buster left town, cops gave him
twenty-four hours to get out.
Told that Indian to go back
to the reservation."

"Flower was up, says he's working."
"Unbelievable."

"I don't really know much myself."
"Nobody does, I guess."

"You go to school, Susan?"
"No. Haven't been to school
for a long time."
"Good girl."

"You got a cigarette?"
"Yeah, sure."
Lit up, pulled smoke in deeply.
"Thanks."
And etcetera small talk,
pinon wood coals crackling.

They were on the way to Monument Valley.
"If you can, climb up on Black Mountain,"
I told them, "and look north. Wow!
you'll see all of Monument Valley,

> *I can see it, the red and brown monoliths*
> *reaching for God, the ocean dried up*
> *just a couple million years ago,*
> *the fish are still squiggling in solid rock,*
> *the footprints of gods are still fresh.*

or you can look south from the Utah side.
It might rain, and it will look all fresh and new.

> *Crawling out of primordial swamp,*
> *the gods' children, look, look—*
> *they are coming.*

"If you can, drive by Canyon de Chelly.
You ever been there? Take a long look
at the Lukachukai cliff face at evening,
the purple and the blue changing,
the evening of a day before another new day."

*I get lonesome talking and thinking about it,
and I stop.*

After a while, Susan and Marge say goodnight.
"We've got to get up early to leave."

"Goodnight."

The last of the firelight dimmed away
and the Milky Starway swept so quietly by
and so far away.

Brothers and Friends

Laugh at Magpie this morning.
He was telling stories
all morning at the top
of his lungs, sitting on a nearby pine.

Magpie, you clown. Longtail,
you surely act goofy.
Get a job, be a good American.
Hey, it's good to laugh with you,
to enjoy the life.

Had a visit from Skunk last night.
He went and ate my last bit of butter
and put trash into some juice.
And then he must have gotten
into the tuna casserole
I was saving for lunch.
Ah well, hope he didn't get sick.

Owl, a lone, hollow wood sound.
The night, windborne,
echoed upon itself.
Several nights ago was
the first time I heard it again.
I got frightened, worried.
And last night, Owl again,
but at peace now, the sound
was a welcome meaning.
I thought about the wind, echoes,
earth, origin, prayer wings.

Magpie.
Skunk.
Owl.
All are my brothers and friends.

A San Diego Poem: January-February 1973

The Journey Begins

My son tells his aunt,
"You take a feather,
and you have white stuff in your hand,
and you go outside,
and you let the white stuff fall to the ground
That's praising."

In the morning, take cornfood outside,
say words within and without.
Being careful, breathe in and out,
praying for sustenance, for strength,
and to continue safely and humbly,
you pray.

Shuddering

The plane lifts off the ground.
The shudder of breaking from earth
gives me a splitsecond of emptiness.
From the air, I can only give substance
and form to places I am familiar with.
I only see shadows and darkness
of mountains and the colored earth.

The jet engines drone heavily.
Stewardesses move along the aisles.
Passengers' faces are normally bland,
and oftentimes I have yearned, achingly,
for a sharp, distinctive face, someone
who has a stark history, even a killer
or a tortured saint, but most times
there is only the blandness.

25

I seek association with the earth.
I feel trapped, fearful of enclosures.
I wait for the Fasten Seat Belt sign
to go off, but when it does
I don't unfasten my belt.

The earth is red in eastern Arizona,
mesa cliffs, the Chinle formation
is an ancient undersea ridge lasting
for millions of years.
I find the shape of whale still lingers.
I see it flick gracefully by Sonsela Butte
heading for the Grand Canyon.

I recite the cardinal points of my Acoma life,
the mountains, the radiance coming
from those sacred points, gathering
into the center.
I wonder: what is the movement
of this journey in this jet above the earth?

Coming into L.A. International Airport,
I look below at the countless houses,
row after row, veiled by tinted smog.
I feel the beginnings of apprehension.
Where am I? I recall the institutional prayers
of my Catholic youth but don't dare recite them.
The prayers of my native selfhood
have been strangled in my throat.

The Fasten Seat Belt sign has come back on
and the jet drone is more apparent in my ears.
I picture the moments in my life
when I have been close enough to danger
to feel the vacuum prior to death
when everything stalls.
The shudder of returning to earth
is much like breaking away from it.

26

NORTHEAST NEBRASKA TECHNICAL
COMMUNITY COLLEGE - LIBRARY

Under L.A. International Airport

Numbed by the anesthesia of jet flight,
I stumble into the innards of L.A. International.
Knowing that they could not comprehend,
I dare not ask questions of anyone.
I sneak furtive glances at TV schedule consoles
and feel their complete ignorance of my presence.
I allow an escalator to carry me downward;
it deposits me before a choice of tunnels.
Even with a clear head, I've never been good
at finding my way out of American labyrinths.
They all look alike to me. I search
for a distinct place, a familiar plateau,
but in the tunnel, on the narrow alley's wall,
I can only find bleak small-lettered signs.
At the end of that tunnel, I turn a corner
into another and get the unwanted feeling
that I am lost. My apprehension is unjustified
because I know where I am I think.
I am under L.A. International Airport,
on the West Coast, someplace called America.
I am somewhat educated, I can read and use a compass;
yet the knowledge of where I am is useless.
Instead, it is a sad, disheartening burden.
I am a poor, tired wretch in this maze.
With its tunnels, its jet drones, its bland faces,
TV consoles, and its emotionless answers,
America has obliterated my sense of comprehension.
Without this comprehension, I am emptied
of any substance. America has finally caught me.
I meld into the walls of that tunnel
and become the silent burial. There are no echoes.

Survival This Way

Survival, I know how this way.
This way, I know.
It rains.
Mountains and canyons and plants
grow.
We travelled this way,
gauged our distance by stories
and loved our children.
We taught them
to love their births.
We told ourselves over and over
again,
"We shall survive this way."

Like myself, the source of these narratives is my home. Sometimes my father tells them, sometimes my mother, sometimes even the storyteller himself tells them.

"I don't know how it started,
but this is the story:

                    One time,
the Kawaikamehtitra—the Laguna people—
were having a rabbit hunt.
Tchaiyawahni ih—in Acoma that means
'hunting and killing each other.'
Among them was an Acoma
who was an in-law to the Lagunas.

At the beginning of the hunt,
the Field Chief gives instructions and bids
the people to pay heed to the rules
and to be careful not to harm each other.
He called to the people,
'Now, you can go out and hunt,
but you must be especially careful
that you don't kill Coyote because
some of you are clan relatives of his.'
There were some Coyote clan people in the hunt.
And he repeated,
'You can kill anything but don't kill Coyote.'

And so the Lagunas and the one Acoma
set out to hunt.
They went out like they do,
encircling the rabbits,
finding and killing them until at one point,
suddenly, Coyote was rousted out
from under a rock ledge
and he ran in the direction of the Acoma.
And the Acoma killed him.

One of the Coyote clan relatives saw it,
and he called, 'Coyote People, Coyote People,
our relative has been killed.
Come here, come here, our poor beloved relative
has been killed by this Acoma.'
And the Coyote People came and they mourned
their relative who was laid out at their feet.
They looked at the Acoma, and they cried angrily,
'Sthuudzhishu Acumeh eh, ahrhehmah,' meaning
'You confounded no-good dirty Acoma.'
And they began to chase him towards Acoma.
But while the Coyote People were chasing
and hollering at the Acoma,
Coyote suddenly jumped up and he ran away.
The Coyote People stopped chasing and cussing
the Acoma and said that he could come back
and be an in-law to the Lagunas again.

I don't know if the story is true or not,
but that's the story I heard,"
my father said.

Sometimes Coyote is Pehrru.
Sometimes Pehrru is Coyote.
Sometimes they're one and the same.

This one is about Pehrru's wonderful kettle.

One day,
Pehrru was cooking at his camp.
He had a kettle of meat and corn
which he had just taken out of the ashes and coals.
The food had been buried, cooking all day long.
And he put the meat and corn on top
of the ashes and coals.
Just then,
a troop of sandahlrrutitra—soldiers—
came along.
They saw Pehrru busy at cooking,

30

and they saw the kettle,
and they smelled the good food.
The kettle was really boiling away,
they could see that, but they didn't see any fire.

"Guwahdze, Pehrru," the soldiers said in greeting.
"Dahwah eh," Pehrru said. He kept on being busy.

"You are sure busy with your cooking,"
the soldiers said.
"Hah uh," Pehrru said.

The soldiers were very curious
about the boiling kettle of stew.
They marvelled at how it was boiling
and there was no fire they could see.

"Your stew is boiling so beautifully,"
the soldiers said.
"Hah uh, it is boiling," Pehrru agreed, casually.

Finally,
curiosity getting the best of them,
the soldiers asked,
"How is it that the stew is boiling
when there is no fire under your kettle?"
Noting their overly anxious curiosity,
Pehrru said, "Oh, it's just that that's the kind
of kettle it is. It boils like that by itself."

"That must be a wonderful kettle,"
the soldiers marvelled.
"Hah uh, it is," Pehrru said, nonchalantly,
"it is quite useful."

The soldiers talked among themselves
and then, without wanting to appear too eager,
they said to Pehrru, "Compadre, do you think
you can give us that wonderful kettle?"
Pehrru kept on being busy at cooking

and then he turned to them and said,
"Tsah dzee wah guwah nehwadi shrouwah drumanoh."

The kettle was really boiling away.
The smell of the meat and corn was delicious.
Indeed it was an amazing, wonderful kettle.
They had to have it, and the soldiers said,
"Well, let us buy the kettle from you."

Pehrru said,
"I don't think I can sell it to you;
it's such a favorite of mine," but he saw
that the soldiers were ready to bargain treasures
for the kettle. He pretended to be less reluctant
to part with his kettle.

They bargained.
The soldiers making an offer
and Pehrru holding back,
the soldiers raising their price
and Pehrru seeming to hold back less and less.
Until the soldiers said,
"We will give you your weight in gold
for the kettle."

And Pehrru, pretending a sorrowful reluctance, said,
"You have made me such a generous offer
for my beloved wonderful kettle, but I think
it is a fair price. Henah, you have bought it."

And the sandahlrrutitra brought Pehrru
his weight in gold and Pehrru gave them
the plain old smoke-blackened kettle
and they rode away . . .

And another one:

                    One time,
four people were eating together.
They saw Pehrru approaching them.
He was coming up the road.

One of them said,
"There comes Pehrru.
Don't anyone invite him to sit down and eat.
He's much of a liar."
The four kept on eating.

Pehrru got to where they were,
and he said, "Guwahzee."
"Dawah eh," they answered,
and they kept on eating.
Nobody invited Pehrru to sit down and eat.

"Wah trou yatawah?" Pehrru asked.
And they answered, "Hah uh, wahstou yatawah."
("Are you eating?"
 "Yes, we're eating.")
Pehrru stood around watching them eat.

To make conversation,
one of the four asked,
"Where are you coming from?"
And Pehrru said,
"Oh, I'm coming from nowhere special."

After a bit more silence, another asked,
"Dze shru tu ni, Pehrru?"
And Pehrru answered,
"Oh, as usual I don't know much of anything."
The four kept on eating
and Pehrru kept standing, watching them eat.

33

And then he said,
"Oh wait, I do know a bit of something,"
and he paused until he was sure
they were waiting for him to go on,
and then he said,
"When I was coming here, I saw some cows."

Pretending to show little interest,
one said, "Oh well, one usually sees
some cows around."

And Pehrru said, "Yes, yes, that's true.
Well, one of them had just given birth
to some calves."

And one of them said,
"Oh well, you know, usually cows
give birth to calves."

"The cow was feeding her calves,"
Pehrru said.

"Oh well, that's what cows usually do,
feed their calves," one of the four said.

And then Pehrru said,
"The cow had given birth to five calves.
One of them, beloved, was just standing around,
looking hungry, not feeding because
as you know, cows usually only have four nipples."

And the four, realizing the meaning
of Pehrru's story, looked at each other
and said,
"Shtsu dzeshu, Pehrru. Sit down and eat."
Smiling, Pehrru joined them in eating.

When it was time to get a meal,
Pehrru was known to be a shrewd man.

35

How to make a good chili stew—
this one on July 16, a Saturday,
Indian 1971

for all my friends who like it

It's better to do it outside
or at sheepcamp
or during a two or three day campout.
In this case, we'll settle
for Hesperus, Colorado
and a Coleman stove.

Ingredients

Chili (Red, frozen, powdered, or dry pods. In this case,
just powdered because that's all I have.)
Beef (In this case, beef which someone who works in a
restaurant in Durango brought this morning,
leftovers, trim fat off and give some to the dog
because he's a good guy. His name is Rex.)
Beef bullion (Five or six cubes, maybe, for taste.)
Garlic (About two large cloves. Smell it to know it's good.)
Salt and pepper (You just have to test how much.)
Onion (In this case, I don't have any, but if you do have
some around, include it with much blessings.)
Hominy (Preferably the homemade kind like we used to make
at home. You soak kernels of corn in limewater
overnight until the husks wash off easy. But
storebought is okay too.)

Directions

Put chile and some water into a saucepan with bullion,
garlic which is diced, and salt and pepper and onion
which I don't have and won't mention anymore because
I miss it and you shouldn't ever be anyplace without it,
I don't care where.

36

And then put it on to barely boiling, cover and smell it
        once in a while with good thoughts in your mind,
        and don't worry too much about it except, of course,
        keep water in it so it doesn't burn, okay.
In the meantime, you can cut the meat (which, in this case,
        I should mention, was meant for Rex the dog but since
        it was left over from just last night and it's not bad—
        I know 'cause I tasted it—that's alright, but if you
        can afford it, cut the lean meat) into less than inch
        pieces and you don't have to measure, just cut it so
        it looks like cut meat.
Make sure you smell the chili in the saucepan once in a
        while and think of a song to go along with it.
        That's important.
More on meat, in the case it's not cooked leftovers from
        last night. Well, you put it into a pan with tiny
        diced garlic with a small pat of butter and meat fat
        and watch it turn brown and listen to it sizzle—
        a delightful sound—for as long as you want just so
        it doesn't burn and set aside and relax for a while.
Smelling and watching are important things, and you really
        shouldn't worry too much about it—I don't care
        what Julia Childs says—but you should pay the utmost
        attention to everything, and that means the earth,
        clouds, sounds, the wind. All these go into the cooking.
And then you put everything into a pot—a cast iron one
        is best, like the one my Dad and I put a sheep's head
        into at sheepcamp with rice and pieces of bread dough
        for dumplings and buried it in the ashes and coals
        so it was cooked by the time we got back to camp in the
        evening from herding sheep.

Further Directions To Make Sure It's Good

Don't forget about the chili.
Look all around you once in a while. (In this case,
        the La Plata Mountains in southern Colorado. It's
        going to rain soon on them and maybe here too
        if we're lucky.)

Don't let the Magpies get on your nerves. (Which is the
        case here because Edward and Susan Magpie's kids
        are here all by themselves. Ed and Su went someplace,
        maybe on vacation or to the big city—Relocation
        Welding School—and the kids are getting into all
        kinds of mischief. I throw them apples once in a
        while, but they're sassy and onery, chattering
        and swearing and laughing all the time, acting big.
        If you see Ed and Su, please tell them everything's
        right on, their kids are getting big and you tell them
        to write. Maybe you'll see them around Oakland or
        Los Angeles, at the Indian Center.
If there are Magpies around, make sure you invite them,
        saying, "I want you all to come over for dinner.
        We've been wondering how you've all been.
        Your Aunts and Uncles and Grandfather will be
        there." Say it with great welcoming and sincerity
        and I'll betcha they'll come.

Waiting For It To Get Done

Oh, maybe about two hours for the chili to simmer
        and then put in the hominy and cover with water
        and simmercook for another two hours.

        It's also good to have someone along,
        and in case they don't know how too good
        you can teach them, slowly and surely,
        until they're expert. It will take more than
        one time but that's okay and much better.
        It's best to do anytime.

At Last

Well, my friends, that's all there is to it,
        for the chili stew part, but as you well know
        there is more than that too. So good luck.
        And you can eat now.

And there is always one more story. My mother
was telling this one. It must be an old story but
this time she heard a woman telling it at one of
those Sunday meetings. The woman was telling
about her grandson who was telling the story
which was told to him by somebody else. All
these voices telling the story, including the voices
in the story—yes, it must be an old one.

One time,
(or like Rainy said, "You're sposed to say, 'Onesa ponsa
time,' Daddy")

there were some Quail Women grinding corn.
Tsuushki—Coyote Lady—was with them.
                                                    She was
grinding u-uuhshtyah—juniper berries.
I don't know why she wasn't grinding corn too—
that's just in the story.

It was a hot, hot day, very hot,
and the Quail Women got thirsty,
and they decided to go get some water to drink.
They said,
          "Let's go for a drink of water,
and let's take along our beloved comadre."
So they said, "Comadre, let's all go
and get some water to drink."
                              "Shrow-uh,"
Coyote said.

The water was in a little cistern
at the top of a tall rock pinnacle
which stands southeast of Acu.
                              They walked
over there but they had to fly to get to the top.

The Quail Women looked at Tsuushki who couldn't fly
to the top because she had no feathers,
                              and they felt
very sorry and sad for Tsuuschki.

So they decided, "Let us give shracomadre
some of our feathers."
                              The Quail Woman said that
and they took some feathers out of themselves
and stuck them on Coyote.
                              And then they all flew
to the top of the pinnacle where the water was.
They all drank their fill and Coyote
was the last to drink.
                              While she was drinking
from the cistern, on her hands and knees,
the Quail Women decided to play a trick, a joke
on Coyote Lady.
                    They said,
"Let's take the feathers from our comadre
and leave her here."
                              "Alright," they all agreed,
and they did that, and they all left.

When Tsuushki had drank her fill of water
and was ready to descend the pinnacle,
she found that she could not
because she had no feathers to fly with anymore.
She felt very bad,
                    and she sat down,
                                        wondering
what to do.
The rock pinnacle was too high up
to jump down off of.

But, pretty soon,
                    Kahmaasquu Baba—
Spider Grandmother—came climbing over the edge
of the pinnacle to drink water also.
And Coyote thought to herself,

                              Aha,
I will ask my Grandmother to help me off.
She is always a wonderful helpful person.

So Coyote asked,
"Dya-ow Kahmaasquu, do you think you could help me
descend this pinnacle? You are always such a
wonderful helpful person."

And Spider Grandmother said,
                              "Why yes,
beloved one, I will help you.
Climb into my basket."
                              She pointed at a basket
tied at the end of her rope.
                              And then
she said, "But I must ask you one thing.
While I am letting you down,
you must not look up, not once,
not even just a little bit.
                              For if you do,
I will drop.
And that is quite a long ways down."

"Oh, don't worry about that, Dyaa-ow,
I won't look up. I'm not that kind of person,"
Coyote promised.
                   "Alright then,"
Spider said, "Climb in
and I will let you down."

The basket began to descend,
                              down
                                        and
                                                  down,
BUT on the way down,
                   Coyote looked up
(At this point, the voice telling the story
is that of the boy who said,
                   "But Tsuushki

41

looked up and saw her butt!")
and Spider Grandmother dropped the basket
and Coyote went crashing down.

Well, at this point, the story ends but,
as you know, it also goes on.
                              Well, sometime later,
the Shuuwimuu Guiguikuutchah—
Skeleton Fixer—came along.
He saw a scatter of bones at the foot of the pinnacle.
Skeleton Fixer said,
                    "Oh look,
some poor beloved one must have died.
I wonder who it may be?"
                              The bones
were drying white in the sun, lying around.
And Skeleton Fixer said,
                    "I think I will put
the bones together
and find out and he will live again."

And he joined the bones together,
                              very carefully,
and when he had finished doing that,
he danced around them while he sang,

"Shuuwimuu shuuwimuu chuchukuu
  Shuuwimuu shuuwimuu chuichukuu
  Bah Bah."
            (which is to say)
  Skeleton skeleton join together
  Skeleton skeleton join together
  Bah Bah.
            And the skeleton bones did,
and the skeleton jumped up,
and it was Coyote.

"Ah kumeh, Tsuushkitruda," Skeleton Fixer said.
Oh, it's just you Coyote—I thought
it was someone else.

And as Coyote ran away,
Skeleton Fixer called after her,

                   "Nahkeh-eh,
bah aihatih eyownih trudrai-nah!"
Go ahead and go, may you get crushed
by a falling rock somewhere!

2

Notes for My Child

Grand Canyon Christmas Eve 1969

(Later to lie down and sleep,
the earth—surrounded by trees—
for my bed.)

The fire is a higher blue
rhythm and melody.
The mist fills the carved earth.
Breathe: who did this?
River. That little river?
And time and wind and birds
and lizards, coyote, the whole earth
spirit of all those things.
Breathing the earth!

My son cries.
I hear him
in the forest.
He's snuggled down
like he was back
on Siberian ice,
the glacial winds howling.
O the stars
O the moon
O the earth
the trees the ground
we have come to pay respect
to you, my mother earth,
who makes all things
bless me
we are humble
bless my sons
make them strong
bless my wife
give her that subtle timelessness

of stones and mist and beauty
the strength
bless me who prays
awestruck.

Shake the log
and the fire flares up
into stars.
Watch the moon
for the earth's time
when it doesn't need time.
Moon sets in the crotch
of a pinon and the forest
is full of smoke.

Go to gather wood,
fall down once
on stones and damp sand,
arms are tired,
breathe heavily.
Peel and cut potatoes,
cut mutton arm
and put fat in the pan.
Put the mutton in,
give Raho some bread.
He wants meat.
Tell him gently to wait.
Get water for coffee,
rake out coals,
drink water which tastes
of mountain and roots,
put the pot
on coals to boil.
Wait.

Mutton sizzles in pan.
Pick out a coal
fallen into the meat.
Damn, the fire is hot,
pain on knuckles,

lick them with tongue.
Evening is getting colder.
Mutton smells good,
put in sliced potatoes,
sizzles, push coals
under the pan.
Wait.
Hunger mumbles in my belly.
And then everything is ready.
Toast bread on fork end.
But one more thing.
Feed the gods some bread,
meat, salt into the fire,
saying, Thank you, eat
with us.
And we eat, finally.

Mutton gets cold too fast.
Grease smoke from fat bits
I threw in the fire
smells good.
The pine wood fire
is a bit too hot
but it's good,
eating by the canyon,
the forest all around.

Nearby a U.S. Forest Service
sign reads:

KAIBAB NATIONAL FOREST
CAMP ONLY IN CAMPING AREAS
NO WOOD GATHERING
GO AROUND OTHER SIDE OF ENCLOSED AREA
&
DEPOSIT 85 CENTS FOR WOOD

This is ridiculous.
You gotta be kidding.
Dammit, my grandfathers

ran this place
with bears and wolves.
They even talked
with each others about it,
and you don't even listen.

And I got some firewood
anyway from the forest,
mumbling, Sue me.

The moon clock has moved
into the higher branches.
Stars cluster
in the pine tops.
I lie down on my earth bed.
Here it is possible
to believe legend,
heros praying on mountains,
making winter chants,
the child being born Coyote,
his name to be the Christ.
Here it is possible
to believe eternity.

My Children

Raho and I watched
a cabinet maker working
at wood.
His hands' movements
shifted wood
around easily, carefully,
knowing just the moment
to put wood to moving saw.
The smell of burnt,
hot wood and slight sweat.
"My son wanted to watch
you working at wood,"
I told the man.
The man looked up briefly,
nodded his head, his hands
stopping only a second.
Raho watching, watching.

Rainy and I watch
sparrows out the window.
They grub in damp earth,
looking for worms, beetles.
Rainy squeals.
"Like a little bird,"
one of my nieces said
on Easter Sunday.
One bird hops into a puddle,
ruffles its feathers,
pokes beak into the water
and shakes its head.
Rainy looks at me.
"A little bird," I tell her.

Speaking

I take him outside
under the trees,
have him stand on the ground.
We listen to the crickets,
cicadas, million years old sound.
Ants come by us.
I tell them,
"This is he, my son.
This boy is looking at you.
I am speaking for him."

The crickets, cicadas,
the ants, the millions of years
are watching us,
hearing us.
My son murmurs infant words,
speaking, small laughter
bubbles from him.
Tree leaves tremble.
They listen to this boy
speaking for me.

This Magical Thing

This, my son
moves his legs,
turns a circle
once
and then again,
a couple more times.
He stops,
looks at me
and laughs
for my approval
of this magical thing
he has done.

I laugh my happiness,
loving him,
loving the magic
of his movement,
of his laughter.
His eyes
look for my eyes,
find me
growing strong.

Notes For My Child

July 5, 1973, when she was born

Wake slow this morning.

Hear Joy moan,
stir around,
and get up sometime after five.

Bit of morning light.

Get up and wash,
put on two days-old coffee.

Later,
we walk for you
over to University Drug.

Sun slants
through trees,
cool morning.

See two cicadas.
One is dead,
the other is buzzing
trying to take off
from the sidewalk.

I want to turn back
and help it
to fly again,
but I realize
the inevitable.

Yesterday,
while chopping weeds,
I uncovered two chrysalis,
the cicadas within them
curled, soft yet.

We get to the hospital.
The taxi driver says, "Goodluck."
"Okay, thanks." Smiling nervous.

Hospitals are consistent.
Crummy. We wait
for someone to notice us.

I tell Joy
to make herself visible.
She can't be anymore visible
she thinks than now,
her belly sticking out.

I ask where my wheelchair is
when Joy gets in hers
and is pushed down the hall
and into an elevator
by a fat unsmiling aide
who doesn't think
I am funny at all.

Upstairs and down a hall,
and Joy disappears
behind some doors.

I squat on the tile floor,
remember a poem Joy has written
about the story teller.

The aide walks by.
She smiles this time
and says, "Okay."
I say, "Okay," too.

Seven other people wait
and make small talk.
A couple of women
are rolled by.

I smile at the six women
and one guy.
A couple smile back.

When the women roll by
everything becomes somber
and slow.

... the Wisconsin Horse
is silent, looks across
the chainlink fence,
the construction going on
a mile away ...

Finally,
I get to join Joy.
She's getting anxious.
Can tell in her eyes,
movements, tremble
about her mouth.

A nurse tells me
to go to Admitting.
A girl asks me a question.
"Are you the responsible party?"
I say, "Yes."
She means money, of course.
Who's going to pay?
I mean I'm the father
of the child bringing life
and continuance.

I go back upstairs.
A woman on the other side
of the room moans a bit,

struggles in her sheets.
An older woman holds her hand.

Joy is pretty relaxed,
takes deep breaths
to make it easier.
Amazing how anyone can relax
at the eve of birth—
only a step along the way,
of course.
I ask Joy if it hurts,
realize it's a dumb
but important question.

A doctor comes along
and puts a plastic machine
upon Joy's belly
and flicks it on.
The doctor calls it
a doptone and says,
"Don't ask me why it's called that.
I don't know. It runs on batteries."

I call it
steady, gentle beating noises
called flesh, bones, blood,
runs on mysteries, dreams,
the coming child.

I am hungry now
but the hospital atmosphere
prevents any real hunger.
The repressiveness of institutions
has trained my stomach.
Tell myself to relax and say,
"When you come out, child,
let's go dance in a while, okay?"

Look out the window
and see the sun
and the parking lot.

Remember I wanted to write
something about that old dog,
kind of skinny and pathetic,
been hanging around our home
for a while, a week or so,
write a story or poem about it.

And then she was born.

. . . I will tell her
about the Wisconsin Horse . . .

She was born then.

"She's as pretty as a silver dollar,"
said Ed Marlow, a miner
in Eastern Kentucky about Caroline Kennedy.
"She's just plain folks."

Albermarle County Sheriff says,
"We found nekkid women
with nekkid pubic hair offensive."

July 5, 1973 is now and soon enough

You come forth
the color of a stone cliff
at dawn,
changing colors,
blue to red,
to all the colors of the earth.

Grandmother Spider speaks
laughter and growing
and weaving things and threading them
together to make life to wear,
all these, all these.

You come out, child,
naked as that cliff at sunrise,

shorn of anything
except spots of your mother's blood.
You kept blinking your eyes
and trying to catch your breath.

In five more days,
they will come,
singing, dancing,
bringing gifts,
the stones with voices,
the plants with bells.
They will come.

Child, they will come.

Earth and Rain, The Plants & Sun

Once near San Ysidro
on the way to Colorado,
I stopped and looked.

The sound of a meadowlark
through smell of fresh cut alfalfa.

Raho would say,
"Look, Dad." A hawk

sweeping
          its wings

clear through
        the blue
of whole and pure
          the wind
                  the sky.

It is writhing
overhead.
Hear. The Bringer.
        The Thunderer.

Sunlight falls
through cloud curtains,
a straight bright shaft.

It falls,
        it falls
    down
    to earth,
a green plant.

Today the Katzina come.
The dancing prayers.
Many times, the Katzina.
The dancing prayers.
It shall not end,
son, it will not end,
this love.

Again and again,
the earth is new again.
They come, listen, listen.
Hold on to your mother's hand.
They come.

O great joy, they come.
The plants with bells.
The stones with voices.
Listen, son, hold my hand.

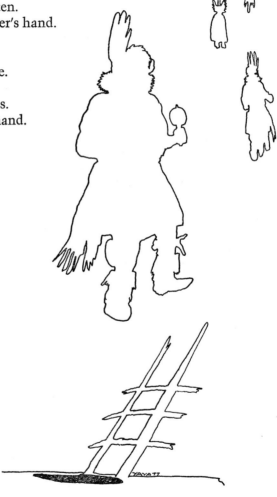

61

Pout

Daughter
sits spraddle-legged
on the floor. Smiles
as she turns the pages
of a catalogue. Toys,
books, clothes, rocky
horseys. Smiles and mur
murs. And then, watching
her, several pages stick
together, and the crinkle
of a frown edges on her fore
head and her lips purse
and push forward in con
cern. And I smile
and pout my mouth
in sympathy and love.

Burning River

I will tell my son over and over again,
"Do not let the rivers burn."
Mountains must stand
until winds and rains come,
and they—and only they—
will cause them to sink
back into the center
of that universal river
which is theirs
and their children's,
Magpie, Bear, and Coyote too.

I will tell him over and over
and over again.

Joan, my hostess, was telling me about the river as she drove
me from Kent State to the airport. "This is the only river in
America that ever burned." The countryside is smalltown
industrial America, settled with small erecto-set plants for
the making of small parts, things to package things in, things
to take things apart with. I am apalled and try to smother
the apprehension that makes me think that soon we shall suffer
many burning rivers.

We wait at the crossing.

The train shudders
with some evil disease.
The disease kills
even as it dies.
And the disease will be
at its furious work
until its frantic energy
will become its burning death.

And then the weakened spirit
will turn to the center
and become the cooled wind
and become the cooled rain
and wash the last vestige
of waste from our bones,
from our charred ligaments
and wash them back

to the River,
the River,
the River,
four times the River.

A Morning Prayer and Advice for a Rainbowdaughter

For this morning:

all around, the everything,
trees, horizons, waters, the animals,
and how one sees, hears, smells,
touches and tastes everything;
these all leading to humility,
        I make myself present,
        facing east.

Feed them, ask for strength, courage,
for it is all theirs,
        I make myself present,
        feeding them.

Beseech the worldspirit, ask for hope
for it comes from there,
        I make myself present.

Recognize the true power, say it
for that is the way,
        I am arriving to myself.

All around, the everything:
        make her all gentle,
        make her all beautiful,
        make her all humble,
        make her a true rainbow daughter,

travelling and seeking and learning and arriving
truly to herself, one with the earth mother
to whom she is kin.

Humbling ourselves, we thank you.

Advice:

learn how to make good bread, being careful and patient
    in everything you do, feeling your making, being gentle
    with the kneading and savoring the result;

enjoy yourself as a child, listen for sounds, let sights
    thrill you incredibly, but do not be demanding,
    inappropriately, of yourself or of others;

pray, in whatever fashion, but always with sincerity
    and with humility;

laugh, o child, learn to and let yourself laugh, always
    as a happy child for honestly enjoyable things;

learn how to recognize sadness, the small and large tragedies,
    coping with them by seeing them in their own true
    perspective so that you may appreciate your own;

respect your parents, brothers and sisters, all your kin,
    friends, and most of all yourself, learn this well;

this is not all, certainly not all, because there is so much
    more, and you will learn that.

Canyon de Chelly

Lie on your back on stone,
the stone carved to fit
the shape of yourself.
Who made it like this,
knowing that I would be along
in a million years and look
at the sky being blue forever?

My son is near me. He sits
and turns on his butt
and crawls over to stones,
picks one up and holds it,
and then puts it into his mouth.
The taste of stone.
What is it but stone,
the earth in your mouth.
You, son, are tasting forever.

We walk to the edge of cliff
and look down into the canyon.
On this side, we cannot see
the bottom cliffedge but looking
further out, we see fields,
sand furrows, cottonwoods.
In winter, they are softly gray.
The cliffs' shadows are distant,
hundreds of feet below;
we cannot see our own shadows.
The wind moves softly into us.
My son laughs with the wind;
he gasps and laughs.

We find gray root, old wood,
so old, with curious twists

in it, curving back into curves,
juniper, pinon, or something
with hard, red berries in spring.
You taste them, and they are sweet
and bitter, the berries a delicacy
for bluejays. The plant rooted
fragilely into a sandy place
by a canyon wall, the sun bathing
shiny, pointed leaves.

My son touches the root carefully,
aware of its ancient quality.
He lays his soft, small fingers on it
and looks at me for information.
I tell him: wood, an old root,
and around it, the earth, ourselves.

Baby Bird Prayers for My Children, Raho and Rainy

watching little birds learning
to fly, Spring 1975, SE Colorado

1

Gentle murmurs of wind, now,
be warm and soothing
to these little ones, this morning
and for all days of this world,
I offer my thoughts and prayers.

2

Be kind, sun, gentle.
I am yet small, my heart beats
with the fragile cycle of the universe.
Be kind, bright sun.
I feel your kindness upon me.
Make me grow tall and strong.

3

This morning, the rush
of my mother's wings
startles me.
Waking to coldness,
I shriek and I shriek.
The noises awaken me even more.
They penetrate to the hunger
I feel and I shriek again.
My mother returns,

69

gently gliding into home.
She feeds me from her mouth.
She leaves, and I shriek
and I shriek again with love
and hunger and growing.

4

Protect these little things.
They are mere blood, bone,
muscle, and they are filled yet
with delicate dreams.
Their spirits are growing
and I want them to know
they come from the rhythm
that the universe is.
Please protect these little ones
and keep them and they will grow
well and rich with life.

5

Little fluff of feathers
alight softly unto the ground.
They welcome you, the soil,
the grass, the little seeds,
the countless insects.
You have fallen from the sky,
the trees, the white clouds.
Little Friends, they say.
You are welcome with us.
We are growing too
and we shall grow together.

6

Put your thoughts in mine,

your small hands, your dreams
with mine and walk with me.
I shall show you a few things.
I shall tell you a few names.
I shall keep you with me
for a while.
I will teach you
for a while.
And then you will fly.
You will fly.

Between Albuquerque and Santa Fe

I told a friend that I was writing what follows below.
We were drinking some good red wine at his home on Cerro
Gordo. His blondhair little daughter was crawling around.
Once in a while his wife would rise from her chair and
stir something in a pot. "Fine," Max said. I think I told
someone else too but I forget who. It was a cold winter day,
getting to evening. I had heard someone mention during that
day that it would snow that night. "I think that's a good
idea," he said.

Fingers Talking In The Wind

They talked,
laughed by making motions,
these children,
their voices.

The wind slowed down;
the Jemez and Sandia Mountains
shrieked their joy.

The children had gotten on the bus
in Santa Fe for Albuquerque,
about a dozen of them.

A Santo Domingo man
sat at the front of the bus.
He didn't say anything,
and he looked straight ahead.

Three teenage girls
from San Felipe Pueblo
were on their way home.

They giggled and laughed
and drank pop and ate cornchips.

I was on my way home.
All of us were on our way home.

One time, this friend who is a cowboy liked this girl very
much. In fact, he loved her then. Another friend told
me the story. This was during my friend's drinking period.
One night, he got wild and lonesome. He went to the girl's
house. She lived in a two-story house. With his lariat,
roped the chimney and hoisted himself up. All of a sudden,
the girl heard a tapping on her bedroom window, and she
looked and saw it was this guy. She laughed and let him in
because it was cold outside and gave him a sandwich
and some orange juice. Just like in the stories, that
one. Don't ever tell him that one, though.

Like Mississippi

Several years back,
Shirley, Rand, Hilary,
Agnes, Brian, Raho and I
were on our way to Taos
just to look around, visit.

We were driving up
the La Bajada south of Santa Fe.
The clay is red there
and Shirley said,
"Just like Mississippi,"
and I said, "Yes, it is."

Further up the La Bajada
and looking west you can see
the land where a fence divides it.
One is Santo Domingo land;
the other side is a U.S. politician's.

73

One side is graybrown dry land
from overgrazing;
the other side is silvery
from replanting and money.

When you get to the top of La Bajada,
you can see the Sangre de Christo,
the Jemez, the Ortiz,
and the Sandia Mountains.
They are all strong and silent.

That day, our two families
took photos as we held our arms
around each others shoulders.

This was the time I was a student at St. Catherine's Indian
School in Santa Fe, when we all went to pick apples in an
orchard in Teseque. That was the first year I was ever away
from home.

We all piled into large trucks in the morning and rode up
there. It's not too far. We picked apples and once in a
while sneaked quick bites. We laughed and joked and teased
the girls. In the break before lunch, the boys went into
the hills and chased rabbits. My cousin almost caught one.

We ran back down to the orchard when they called us for
lunch. The nuns gave us baloney sandwiches and lukewarm
milk and apples for lunch. We picked apples for a short
while after lunch. And then because it was a tradition,
all the boys ran back to the school.

It's about nine miles up a long, long hill, alongside the
highway from Santa Fe and then down a long downsloping
ridge. All the way, there are cedar trees and some pinon. When
everyone got back to the school, we all went into the chapel
and said a prayer for thanks. That was that time.

A New Mexico Place Name

In this case, American history
has repeated itself.
It is too easy to stop itself.

COCHITI CITY

The crux is a question
of starving or eating.
An unfair question, surely
but who of the people
will not find it necessary
to ask?

Salas, of the old city,
points his finger
toward the
                CITY
off to the right,
pointing to where
there is a sacred place.
"Right there," he says,
a halting in his voice,
"right there,"
and a bulldozer rumbles
over the horizon
of the hill unto that place.

This year a model

CITY

is being sold by salesmen
from Southern California.
Sometimes I think
that history will come
to know no one
except its salesmen.

Sam, Jody, and I went to see the model city in June 1971.
I had just hitched back from North Carolina. Armed with
a tape recorder and questions, we went up there. Sam took
a photo of the sign: COCHITI CITY.

The U.S. Corps of Engineers were busy. Their heavy machines
were incessant. There were some pipelines and sprinklers
in operation. There was no grass in sight. The steel blades
had taken care of that. The ground was bone bare.

We went to the sales office and stood around, arrogant young
men, anxious and nervous, and then we asked for the manager.
Someone led us to his office. He stood up, smiling, cool,
and shook hands with us and invited us to sit down. Sam
paced the floor like a mountain lion.

The man punched a button on his intercom and spoke into it.
A pudgy man came with a sheaf of brochures and forms under
his arm. He passed them all around. Sam refused the hand-
out. We asked questions and Jody turned on his tape recorder.
It was incongruous, of course. Three Indians, young and
angry, bantering with two whitemen who represented millions
of dollars from somewhere, asking insistent questions which
had no chance, realistically, of being answered.

We stayed only as long as Sam could stand it—he paced all
that time—and before he lunged at that smiling salesman.
We laughed and tried to talk with a Cochiti man who was watering some shrubbery foreign to the land. One of the
salesmen called to him and he went over and then around the
corner of a building. A pretty Indian girl at the reception
desk refused to talk with us. We left.

On the way from COCHITI CITY, we saw several Indian men
digging at a big hole in the ground. We waved to them.
Sam took a photo and said he would title it, "Indians
Building a New Way of Life." We didn't wonder what was to
fill in the hole. It wasn't a strange feeling at all that
there wasn't much to say. We stopped at Pena Blanca for a
half pint and a six-pack. On the way back to Albuquerque,
we drank in silence.

76

NORTHEAST NEBRASKA TECHNICAL
COMMUNITY COLLEGE · LIBRARY

Back Into the Womb, The Center

We got into Dave's VW
in Albuquerque and drove
for Cochiti Canyon,

past the village, on a dirt road
unto a mesa which very gently
upsloped, and Dave pointed
to a distant white space of clay,
saying, "Right there is the beginning."

At the mouth
the canyon begins without notice.
It's just jumbles of rock.
The canyon walls become higher
and you don't notice at all
that you're going deeper in.

It's higher then,
you can tell by the oak
and soon the ponderosa.
The air is cooler
and suddenly there is a fish hatchery
and a couple of buildings
painted like the US Game & Fish Dept.
We passed on by, rising,

until about a mile up, again suddenly,
we came upon a small, clear dam
surrounded by huge boulders,
and we stopped.

I found that the dam
is a natural one,
caused by an ancient rockslide,
and then I looked up
and the immensity of the place
settled upon me without weight.
I knew that we were near

one of the certain places
that is the center of the center.
Later on, when I walked
a mile up, I found the crotch
where the canyon enters
the mountain, the crotch
where there is a clump
of thick brush, and I felt cold.

It is strange this time,
and I have to pray this way.
"Do you mind if I sit on this stone
and lean against this mountain
and listen to the silence of everything?
Do you mind if I go back 10,000 years?"

My mother and my father took me away to school that time.
We got on the train in Grants. My father worked for the
AT&SFRY railroad at that time, he had a pass which we could
use to go most anywhere the railroad went. This time it was
to Santa Fe but the railroad only got as far as Lamy and from
there we had to ride the bus into town.

The way we went was this way. From Grants past our home in
McCartys where my mother said, "There's our home. Look."
I looked but tears blurred my eyes, the train noise was heavy
on my ears. And then Laguna, past Mesita, burning southeast
for Belen where the train turns north for Albuquerque. From
Albuquerque past the pueblos of Sandia, Bernallio, Algodones,
San Felipe, and Santo Domingo. And then unto the Galisteo
uplift from where you can see the largest mountains of the
southern Rockies, the Sandias, Jemez, and the Sangre de Cristo.
The train goes on the uplift until almost to Lamy where it
flattens out and is like that until the train slows down and
stops at the depot. We got out with a few other people and
got on the bus for Santa Fe.

It was almost dark by then and became really dark by the time
we got into the city. My father tried to cheer me up by telling

funny stories of the time he went to school in Santa Fe. We stayed at the De Vargas Hotel that night. My father said he had to go get some cigarettes. It was during Santa Fe Fiesta that time. He was gone for two hours and when he came back I was still awake and he was singing under his breath and I could hear him talk soothingly to my mother.

The next morning we all walked up to the school. On the way up there my father bought us a bag of Nambe peaches and we ate them on the way. The nuns at Saint Catherines Indian School seemed to be waiting for me and they patted me on my shoulder and said that Mass was about to begin. We all went into the chapel. During a lull in the service, when everything was quiet except for the priest moving silently about the altar, I fainted.

I just fainted, that's all, into the subtle chasm that opens and you lose all desire and control, and I fell, very slowly, it seemed. I found myself being carried out by my father to some steps in front of the boys recreation hall. He talked with me for a long time, slowly and gently, and I felt him tremble and stifle his sobs several times. He told me not to worry and to be strong and brave.

I wonder if I have been. That was the first time I ever went away from home. It's a memory of it, that time.

A Birthday Kid Poem

Don't worry about the pain
at the upper part of your hip.
Bone and flesh are ephemeral
in the count of centuries after all,
and your life is intermittent.

Prefer to consider eternity
at least; that way you know
that things continue the way
that life has been, a constant motion
gathering everything from the outer limits
of the universe—wherever those are—
into the core of the universe—
wherever that it—and all through the motion
which is time and sequences
you are passing through.

Consider that instead and love
yourself well and appropriately.
Love your children and love your kinfolk.
Love the mothers of your children.
Love the small things.
Love the big things.
Love things in the manner that they should be loved.
Be strong, humble, clear in vision,
and do not dream so fantastically
that you lose the reality
that dreams are,
that they are signals and roads
by which to guide the reality
of all the days that you are going through.

Believe that things will end well
for you; believe that things
will end well for all things.

Believe that hope is useful
even if sometimes it seems useless.
Believe, o man, o god, believe.

Be cool now.
Think of Coyote.
Think of Magpie.
Think of Raho Nez and Rainy Dawn.
Think of all the things you love.
Think peace and humility
and certainty and strength.

It shall end well.
It shall continue well.
It shall be.
It shall.
It shall.
It shall.
It shall.

That's the way things continue.
Emeh eh eh ka aitetah.
That's the way that things become.
Emeh eh eh naitra guh.

Quumeh.
Hahtrudzaimeh.
Like a woman.
Like a man.

Nyow skhetsashru.
Endure.
Nyuu skhetsashru.
Be enduring.
BE ENDURING.

3

How Much
He Remembered

Woman, This Indian Woman

1

O, I miss you so lonely.
Aiiee, it aches.

The black mountain.
The black crow.
Long black hair.

She came riding
over a small hill,
from behind a cedar tree
and faced me.

Her eyes are deep,
the history
of long dreams,
into me.

A small creek by Tsailee,
a small girl
drives her sheep by.

It's so long a time,
a lonely word
without you,
alone.

2

Her brown hands touched
his face, the breath drawn
out from his life,

her hands trembling,
a last giving so close
to life it is near birth.

Eyes touch: lover, I remember
the quick lights moving.
Hair touch: man, my fingers
pushed smoothly upon.
Teeth touch: boy, I fed you
to grow, to run, to vibrate.
Face touch: Sun, it was I held
out my hands, my body to receive.

3

When she laid down,
she was conceived.

When she gave birth,
she was glad for her son.

When the boy asked,
she said, "The sun, your father."

When she died,
the earth remembered her well.

4

I remember her well.

Watching Salmon Jump

It was you:
I could have crawled
between mountains—
that is where seeds are possible—
and touched the soft significance
of roots of birth and the smell of newborn fish

        and

know how it is
leaping into rock
so that our children may survive.

Some Indians At a Party

"Where you from?"

Juneau
Pine Ridge
Sells
Tahlequah
Salamanca
Choctaw
Red Lake
Lumbee
Boston
Wind River
Nambe
Ft. Duchesne
Tesuque
Chinle
Lame Deer
Seattle
Pit River
Brighton Res
Vancouver
Parker
Acoma
the other side, ten miles from Snow Bird.

That's my name too.

Don't you forget it.

Places We Have Been

Vada's in Cuba, New Mexico

I wrote her a small poem about this.
She sent me back a zerox copy, wrote,
"thought you might like to have a copy."
I wouldn't mind having copies
of all the things I've ever done.

Vada's is a dark, cool roadside bar
on a slow spring day, hot outside.
We'd turned back this side of Nageezi,
been going somewhere we never got to,
and we stopped in for a drink.
I ordered a whiskey shot and beer,
and she was drinking beer.

Old man Chicano bartender there,
we liked him and he liked us.
He spoke German from the War,
and she spoke French. An old man Jemez,
friend of bartender, was there too.
He spoke Navajo. I spoke Acoma.
We were a confluence of separate languages
and the common language of ourselves.

We flipped a quarter for music
but the bartender said, "Forget it,"
smiled and put his coins in the jukebox.
She asked, "What are we going to do now?"
"I don't know," I answered.
Maybe we should go someplace.
Yeah, maybe. We drank up,
said goodbye to the old men,
"We'll see you again," and left.

I wonder how they all are
and where we went after we left.

Northern Maine

There was a mountain towards Canada.
I looked at the horizon it was
for a long time because I thought
it looked like Kaweshtima at home
and I had left a couple months back
and was lonely for my son and wife.

We'd driven on narrow roads from Calais.
I was glad they were deserted
and we didn't stop for anything because
I was leery of the white people
being leery of me, a longhaired Indian.
We arrived finally at Moosehead Lake.
We walked on the lakeshore
until we got cold and hungry and found
we had nothing to eat. It was too far
to drive to a store seventeen miles back.
We had come that far, and it was too far
then to go back. We went hungry.

I watched her trying to photograph
a bare twig against the steel gray sky.
I was oblivious to her purpose
and I watched the wind ripple the water
and imagined huge fish in the lake.
She looked at me then, and I helped her
jump ashore safely from a stone.

I woke late that night, late
to a bird cry from across the lake,
a far shore. I saw pine branches
against the black sky. It was too far
then into the night darkness, too far
away from the pinpoints of stars,
and I was too far away, alone.

90

Indianhead Bay

I wrote a poew with Kennebek River
in it, wondering where the hell
all thc Indians had gone to, no sign
of them around. Even I felt foreign.
I had commented, "Not even dried feces left."
Her father said, "There used to be some."

Whose Indian head?—I kept thinking.
Mine I suppose—I kept answering.

Her mother told her she thought I was lazy.
I liked to sleep late, nothing for a
Pueblo Coyote to do there, too far from home,
no sandstone cliffs to build dwellings upon.

We walked down to the Bay.
It scared me because it looked much deeper
than it was, the water moving too slow.
I could barely perceive the seaweed flowing.
I wondered how many Indians there had been.

She showed me a cabin her sister had built.
She was planning on building one too.

I helped her father rake dry brush together
on land he was clearing. It *was* strange,
an Acoma Indian helping a Pilgrim descendent
pile underbrush together to burn.

My head probably as I said.

Ithaca, New York

On the way to Buffalo we got lost.
I got lost a lot that year.
A night freeway this time,
I remembered Vada's, and I asked,
"How far?" "I don't know," she said.

We found a junction bar, a hotel
upstairs, low sleek cars parked outside.
We walked in, asked for a room,
and the hotel night clerk wondered
at us for a long moment, not knowing
what to think of a long-haired Indian
with a white woman asking for a room
at a Black hotel. Tired, I was going
to explain, "I'm just taking her back
to her ship, man, that's all,
give us a damn room."

An ancient elevator took us
to a bare gray room.
I kept worrying about being lost,
kept looking out the window.
"You promised," she said, trying
to reach me. "I know," I said and went
on ahead on a far and wearied bourbon
trip to sleep.

Upstate

Coming from Montreal,
we stopped at a roadside place.
She had to use the restroom
and I stepped into the tavern.
A man, surly white drunk, told me,
"I know an Indian who dances nearby."
He wanted to show me, cursed me
because I was sullen
and didn't want to see.
She came and saved me.
I said, "It's a good thing you're white."
And she was hurt, angry.
It's an old story.
On the wall was a stuffed deerhead,
fluff falling out, blank sad eyes.
We drove madly out of the parking lot

and she didn't say anything
until we finally arrived in Vermont.

We were tired of being in the car,
our bodies and spirits cramped.
We ate in a small town.
We drove to a hillside.
The weather was muggy and hot.
I talked crummy to her, made love,
she cried, I felt sorry and bad.
I get crazy sometimes and impossible
I've heard.
                    It rained hard that night.
The lights of the town below
shimmering through the rain into me.
All night long, I was lonely
and bothered by New England Indian ghosts.

How Much Coyote Remembered

O, not too much.
And a whole lot.

Enough.

Morning By A Lakeside In
Marion County, S.C.

Spring 1970

1

Dear Kathryn and the others,
the young makers and builders
who are called, by them, the anarchists:

I was driving the highway between Pensacola & Atlanta,
not paying much attention to the car radio at all
until on a stretch of dull Interstate asphalt,
a voice shattered boredom like a howitzer.

I stopped and was silent and felt sorrow
eventually, just past a sign which read:
NO PARKING EXCEPT IN CASE OF EMERGENCY.
I climbed a fence and hugged a tree, hoping
to receive forgiveness by loving the earth.

Was it a good place to die,
someplace called Kent State USA?
What period of history is this anyway?

2

Last night old Bullfrog was trying
to make up his mind about his bass,
whether to keep it or throw it away.
Tuning in one last time, all night long.

It's hard to throw old things away.
In the morning, bass strings trembly
and loose, he still hasn't made up his mind.

3

In all my life I never thought
I would spend a night in South Carolina.
But here I am, Marion County. Sandy land
planted with cotton, some soybean, tobacco.
I've seen the white people
and I've seen the Black people.
The whites mainly driving cars,
the Blacks mainly walking.
I've seen the worn gray shacks
and I've seen the ranchstyle homes.
Marion seems like a clean town.
I've even seen a sign reading,
"We always mind our own business."

4

The sun comes red out of clouds
at the far end of the lake.
"Good words and love," Jackson said
in east Texas, talking
about the Alabama-Coushatta way
of saying goodbye.

"We came here," he said, laughing
bitterly, over a case and half of Schlitz,
"in the 1800s. Before that
we owned Georgia, Alabama, and Mississippi."

Woman Dreamer: Slender Oak Woman

A pretty girl lent me some typing paper.
Long ages of Indian in her face; this one
from the north. San Luis Valley, family
of farm workers; beets, onions, lettuce.

At lunch in the line, there was a Mexican
woman pushing a cart of hot food.
She was very dark, high bones in her face,
flashing dark eyes, scar on her upper lip.

> I can imagine you, woman,
> woman, when you were fourteen,
> running towards the mountains.
> You must have had long legs,
> slender oak, running running
> in the wind.

There was another woman I saw in the main
VAH office building. She was drinking
water from the fountain and later I saw her
walking. She reminded me of a woman
I loved for fun. She moved like she laughed,
very sure of herself, teasing, long legs.
She was salmon; fast runner; she was oak
slender woman; Tlingit.

> I can see the oak slender
> woman running the mountainslope.
> The wind flies into her.
> The sky is clear all the way
> to all the horizons.
> She, the slender oak young spring
> of herself, is running running.

96

Apache Love

*Cibecue is on the western edge
of the White Mountain Apache
land in Arizona*

It is how you feel
about the land.

It is how you feel
about the children.

It is how you feel
about the women.

It is how you feel
about all things.

Hozhoni,
in beauty.

Hozhoni,
all things.

Hozhoni,
for all time.

Hozhoni,
through all journeys.

"Those are our White Mountains," Judy said.

"Don't let these old women do all the work for you,"
old man said.

"It makes me feel good, all you young people,"
old woman said.

"It is our own Apache way," Mrs. Early said.

If I ever come back,
it will be through here.

It would be good to ride a horse
through these mountains.

It would be good to stop and rest
by a stone as big as the spirits.

It would be good to go back
and touch the Mountain's people.

Salt River Canyon,
"It's about fifteen miles," Sam said.

Salt River Canyon,
we threw stones into the canyon.

Salt River Canyon,
the mountains, the canyons all around us.

Apache old woman, gray hair, you in beauty.

Apache woman, black hair, you in beauty.

Apache young girl, strong limbs, you in beauty.

Apache younger girl, growing, you in beauty.

It is you,
it is you,
it is you,
it is you.

Her Story About Saving Herself

The way she tells it
makes me feel wealthy,
thinking about a woman,
her child growing in her,
determined to save herself
by going into the Minnesota woods,
building a home.

> Are you Wolverine Woman?
> Are you the luminescence
> that spirits away when I smile
> recognizing you?

I see her the way
that warmth comes over me
gradually as she dispells
with her words any doubts
I ever had about my life.
Her story holds me true,
and I want to keep on
listening and hearing
and knowing her tell me again.

> Later, Wolverine Woman,
> the moon will be out
> and the silver shadows
> will stand still for me.

Two Coyote Ones

I remember that one about Coyote
coming back from Laguna Fiesta
where he had just bought a silver belt buckle.
He was showing off to everyone.
That Coyote, he's always doing that,
showing off his stuff.
                    Probably,
it wasn't as good as he said it was,
just shiney and polished a lot.
I never saw it myself, just heard about it
from one of his cousins who said
the Navajo was kind of wobbly when Coyote
bought it for five dollars and a small sack
of wheat flour he'd "borrowed"
from a Mesita auntie.
                    That Coyote,
I wonder if he still has that silver buckle
that everyone was talking about
or did he already pawn it at one of those
places "up the line."
He's like that you know and then he'd tell
people who ask,
                    "Well, let me tell you.
I was at Isleta and I was offered
a good deal by this compadre who had
some nice ristras of red chili. He had
a pretty sister . . ." and so on.
And you can never tell.

One night in summer in southern Colorado,
I was sitting by my campfire.
Rex, the dog, was lying down
on the other side of the fire.
                    I could see

100

the lonely flicker of the fire
in his distant eyes.
(That sounds like just talk
but Rex was a pretty human dog.)
                                And this
blonde girl came along. I mean that.
She just came along, driving a truck,
and she brought a cake.
That was real Coyote luck, a blonde girl
and a ginger cake. We talked.
She lived south of my camp some miles,
just past the bridge over the Rio de la Plata.
Her parents and her brothers raised goats.
That's where the money was she said,
and besides goats are pretty-well mannered
if you treat them right.
                      I said, Well
I don't know about that. We used to raise
goats too.
               Coyote doesn't like goats too much.
He thinks they're smartass and showoff.
Gets on his nerves he says.
Goats think pretty much the same of him,
saying,
               Better watch out for that cousin.
He gets too sly for his ownself
to be trusted. He'll try to sell you
a sack of flour that's got worms in it
that somebody probably has thrown out.
                                     And
they'd get into a certain story
about one time at Encinal when he brought
a wheelbarrow that was missing only one wheel
to this auntie he liked and he had a story
for why the wheel was missing . . .
And so on.

Anyway, the girl was nice, her hair shining
in the firelight, nice soft voice.
She told me her name but I forget now.

Said she was going to Boston for med school,
said she liked raising goats but it was time
for her to go East.
                    Actually, we just talked
about the goats and what I was doing
which was living at the foot of the La Plata
Mountains and writing.
                    I think I could have
done something with that gimmicky-sounding
line, which was true besides, but I didn't.
It was just nice to have a blonde girl
to talk with. I had to tell Rex the dog
to cool it a couple of times. He and I
were alone a lot that summer, and we were
anxious but we kept our cool.
When she was leaving I asked her to come
back again. She said she'd like to but
she was leaving for Denver the next day.
Okay then, I said and thanked her
for the ginger cake and the talk.
"Goodbye and goodluck." Yeah, "Goodbye."

There's this story that Coyote was telling
about the time he was sitting at his campfire
and a pretty blonde girl came driving along
in a pickup truck and she . . . And so on.

And you can tell afterall.

4

Will Come Forth in Tongues and Fury

A DESIGNATED NATIONAL PARK

Montezuma Castle in the Verde Valley, Arizona.

DESIGNATED FEDERAL RECREATION FEE AREA
ENTREE FEES
$1.00 FOR 1 DAY PERMIT
MONTEZUMA CASTLE ONLY INCLUDES PURCHASER
OR OTHERS WITH HIM IN PRIVATE NON-COMMERCIAL
VEHICLE
$0.50 FOR 1 DAY PERMIT
MONTEZUMA CASTLE ONLY INCLUDES PURCHASER
ON COMMERCIAL VEHICLE

AUTHORIZED
BY THE LAND AND WATER CONSERVATION FUND
ACT OF 1965

This morning,
I have to buy a permit to get back home.

Birds,
they must have been,
these people.
"Thank you for letting me come to see you."
I tell them that.

Secreted in my cave,
look at the sun.
Shadows on sycamore,
a strange bird and a familiar bird.
River, hear the river.
What it must be,
that pigeon sound.

Hear
in my cave, sacred song.
Morning feeling, sacred song.
We shall plant today.

PRESS BUTTON
(on a wooden booth)
"For a glimpse into the lives
of these people who lived here."

Pressing the button, I find
painted sticks and cloth fragments
in a child's hand,
her eyelashes still intact.
Girl, my daughter, my mother,
softly asleep.
They have unearthed you.

59TH CONGRESS OF THE UNITED STATES OF AMERICA
AT THE FIRST SESSION,
BEGUN AND HELD AT THE CITY OF WASHINGTON
ON MONDAY, THE FOURTH DAY OF DECEMBER,
ONE THOUSAND, NINE HUNDRED AND FIVE.

AN ACT
FOR THE PRESERVATION OF AMERICAN ANTIQUITIES.

And a last sign post quote:

BUILT SOMETIME BETWEEN
1200 AD AND 1350 AD
ABANDONED BY AD 1450.

s/ The Sinagua Indians

SEE MUSEUM FOR MORE INFORMATION

Long House Valley Poem

*the valley is in northeastern Arizona
where one of the largest power centers
in this hemisphere is being built*

Sheep and woman.
The long brown and red land
looming unto the horizon.
                    Breathe in so deeply.

Tsegi,
a canyon.
"Hello" and "Goodbye,"
but always Hello
and smile.

The old rocks, millions of years old.

A Mohawk camper trailer
pulled behind a big white Cadillac.
Tourists,
the crusaders.

A cop car
flashing frenetic orange.
Slowwww down. I can't
even remember my license plate number.

And then, suddenly
the Peabody Coal Company.
Black Mesa Mine.
Open pit.

Power line over the Mountain,
toward Phoenix, toward Denver,

toward Los Angeles, toward Las Vegas,
carrying our mother away.

A sign reads: Open Range.
Bulldozer smoke and dust rise
from the wounded Mountain.

A PLAGUE ON ALL YOUR DAMN HORSEPOWER
A PLAGUE ON YOUR KENNECOTT COPPER BLIGHTS

The old rocks, millions of years old.

Horses quietly grazing, quietly.
A skinny black one throws his head
at the sky, at the wind.

The Yei
and hogans and the People
and roadside flowers
and cornfields and the sage
and the valley peace,
they are almost gone.

Blessings

for Mrs. Aguilar, James, and my son
at a civilrights fundraising function
in 1969

You and your crooked leg, James.
You and your hunger, Mrs. Aguilar.
They are getting bored with your misfortunes.

My son is too young to talk
about what his bones need or how much
his belly might be hurting,
but I am thinking they will be bored
with him too.

"How much gas do you need for a tractor?
For three tractors?" they ask.
"How much would it cost our foundation?"

I wait for them to ask,
"How many dreams have you spent lately?
How many hopes?"

We are not hungry for promises of money
nor for anyone to write us
carefully written proposals.
We are hungry for the good earth,
the deserts and mountains growing corn.
We are hungry for the conviction
that you are our brothers and sisters
who are willing to share our love
and compassionate fingers in your hands.

The grass of this expensive lawn
and the drinks make me feel

a stranger and my acute hunger.
My son smiles while someone says,
"I am not politic; I am talking with you."

Mrs. Aguilar with your orange dress
and plastic flowers, I am asking blessings
for you with prayers for corn and potatoes,
the growing things for your land,
and my son is hoping with his smile
not to be hungry tomorrow.

James, you 1950's pachuco,
you are aching in my throat.
You are the many Indians, the anarchists
rising out of the wine slop, angry,
the ones killing false promises,
fighting cops—we are also seeking
blessings for you, for us, for our children
in this war.

Irish Poets on Saturday And An Indian

We bought each others' drinks,
talked poetry, talked about Welch,
Blackfeet from Montana, good poet,
that Indian chasing lost buffalo
through words, making prayers
in literary journals. Yeah,
strange world, drinking bourbon
and water and then beers. Tony,
one Irish poet, and Sydney,
the other Irish, who laughs deeply
at a name Tony says. Murphy,
Murphy Many Horses, laughing Irish
whiskey Indian, we laugh for the
sound of our laughter.
                    And then,
I tell about the yet unseen translation
where Indians have been backed up into
and on long liquor nights, working
in their minds, the anger and madness
will come forth in tongues and fury.

Ten O'clock News in the American Midwest

Bernstein disc jockey tells
about Indians on the ten o'clock news.
O they have been screwed.

I know everybody talks
about Indians yesterday,
the murdering conquest,
the buffalo bones strewn
across hills in Kansas,
the railroad roaring progress.

Late today or early tomorrow
in ghost dance dreams surely
we will find Bernstein doesn't know
what Indians say these days
in wino translations.
He doesn't know that.
And even Indians sometimes
refuse to know because we fear
the trains and what Bernstein tells us
on the ten o'clock news.

Grants to Gallup, New Mexico

Grants, Okie town,
Texans from the oilfields
come to dig uranium
for Phillips Petroleum.
Milan, mobile home town.
    West,
      semis busting gut, gears snarling.
Sawmill this side of Prewett.
      West for California.
Thoreau, gas station and bar,
Navajos leaning on the walls,
    West, pass on by,
      see you on the way back.
Top of The World,
Real Indian Village,
reptiles, moccasins, postcards 5¢,
restrooms, free water.
Coolidge.
Continental Divide.
North Chavez.
Iyanbito, a Shell Oil Co. Refinery.
    West, you see
      Red Gods emerging from the cliffs
      several miles north
      of the Santa Fe railroad.
      Keep going.
Wingate Army Depot, ammo storage
on the hills, rows and rows
of bunkers, freight cars pulling away
loaded for war, for Vietcong.
    West. A Cadillac
      with a fat white cat
      and a blonde teenybopper.
Church Rock turnoff

where an Indian man waits.
We stop for him and he runs to us.
Where you going?
Gallup.
     West. California is too far.
     Once I been to California.
     Got lost in L.A., got laid
     in Fresno, got jailed in Oakland,
     got fired in Barstow,
     and came home.
Gallup, Indian Capital of the World,
shit geesus, the heat is impossible,
the cops wear riot helmets,
357 magnums and smirks, you better
not get into trouble and you better
not be Indian. Bail's low though.
Indian Ceremonial August 7-10,
the traders bring their cashboxes,
the bars are standing room only
and have bouncers who are mean,
wear white hats and are white.
     West, sometimes I feel like
     going on.
     West into the sun at evening.

The following words are for a white friend who I
was telling about the time, day before New Years
1972, that I helped a Jemez man off the pavement
where he had fallen. The words, also, are for that
Jemez and for me.

I find now
that you have finally
come to know me

or so you say

when I have
followed you
all this time,
following your guilty tracks,
finding all those bodies
strewn along the way.

I have honestly loved
your women,
even been insulted by them,
even as they asked
for forgiveness
trying to prove you guiltless.

Now, you have found me,
shorn naked and ashamed,
cold and shivering,
sprawled at this one corner
of your trackless
American concrete patterns.

I welcome you
anyway and again
to see into me
in order that you may see
yourself.

"And The Land Is Just As Dry"

line from a song by Peter LaFarge

The horizons are still mine.
The ragged peaks,
the cactus, the brush, the hard brittle plants,
these are mine and yours.
We must be humble with them.

The green fields,
a few, a very few,
Interstate Highway 10 to Tucson,
Sacaton, Bapchule,
my home is right there
off the road to Tucson,
before the junction.
On the map, it is yellow
and dry, very dry.
Breathe tough, swallow,
look for rain and rain.

Used to know Ira, he said,
his tongue slow, spit on his lips,
in Mesa used to chop cotton.
Coming into Phoenix from the north,
you pass by John Jacobs Farm.
Many of the people there,
they live in one room shacks,
they're provided for by John Jacobs.
Who pays them $5 per day in sun,
enough for quart of wine on Friday.
Ira got his water alright.
Used to know him in Mesa in the sun.
My home is brown adobe
and tin roof and lots of children,

broken down cars, that pink Ford
up on those railroad ties.
Still paying for it
and it's been two years since
it ran, motor burned out,
had to pull it back from Phoenix.

Gila River, the Interstate sign says
at the cement bridge over bed
full of brush and sand and rusty cans.
Where's the water, the water
which you think about sometimes
in empty desperation?
It's in those green, very green fields
which are not mine.

You call me a drunk Indian, go ahead.

Vision Shadows

Wind visions are honest.
Eagles clearly soar
into the craggy peaks
of the mind.
The mind is full
of sunprayer
and childlaughter.

The Mountains dream
about pine brothers and friends,
the mystic realm of boulders
which shelter
rabbits, squirrels, wrens.
They believe in the power.
They also believe
in quick eagle death.

The eagle loops
into the wind power.
He can see a million miles
and more because of it.

All believe things
of origin and solitude.

     But what has happened
(I hear strange news from Wyoming
of thallium sulphate. Ranchers
bearing arms in helicopters.)
to these visions?
I hear foreign tremors.
Breath comes thin and shredded.
I hear the scabs of strange deaths
falling off.

121

Snake hurries through the grass.
Coyote is befuddled by his own tricks.
And Bear whimpers pain into the wind.

Poisonous fumes cross our sacred paths.
The wind is still.
O Blue Sky, O Mountain, O Spirit, O
what has stopped?

Eagles tumble dumbly into shadows
that swallow them with dull thuds.
The sage can't breathe.
Jackrabbit is lonely and alone
with eagle gone.

It is painful, aiiee, without visions
to soothe dry whimpers
or repair the flight of eagle, our own brother.

Heyaashi Guutah

The diaphanous morning cloud
                                comes
                                        down

from the southwest mesa
from Acu
and into Tsiahma,
passes,
and heads up the wet black road
to Budville.

                    Poor wrecking yard,
                    Baptist Indian Mission,
                    tilted sign dangling
                    over the door to Kings Bar.

That man stumbles
against the lurch in his belly.
The night's terrored sleep
is a reflection in the dark window.
Mud from the ravine
clings to his pants.

                    It's not open yet.

Across the road, a woman waits.

The ghost moves slowly northwards
towards Kaweshtima.
It looks back
and waits for them, patiently.

Time To Kill In Gallup

City streets
are barren
fronts for pain
hobbles toward
Rio Puerco wallow hole
       up under the bridge.
My eyes are pain,
"Yaahteh."
Yesterday
they were visions.
Sometimes my story
has worked
but this time
       the falling scabs
reveal only a toothless
woman.

Gumming back sorrow,
she gags on wine.
One more countless time
       won't matter.
Says,
"One more,
my friend."
I know him, standing,
by the roadside.
He got lost,
"didn't wanna go home,"
       and we left him
a ghost to remember.
Only sorrow has no goodbyes.

These Gallup streets
aren't much

for excuses
            to start on at least
one last goodtime.

"So forgetful,"
it's easy, "you are,"
she said.
            Sweeping her hand,
knocking on cold railroad tie.
She shudders
too often a load
of children bound
to be bound
in rags.

The children
have cried too many times,
would only dig more graves,
lean on church walls.
For warmth,
"Sure why not."
Look for nickles, dimes,
pennies, favors,
            quick cold kisses.
The child whimpers
pain
into gutters.
These streets never
were useful
for anything
except tears.

She rubs her one last eye.
the other is a socket
for a memory
she got ripped,
ripped off
at Liberty Bar,
saving a pint of wine,
thinking she was saving

grace
and would be granted
redemption
if she fought
or turned over
           one more time.

Sister. Sister. These streets
are empty.
They have only told sighs
which are mean
and clutch with cold evil.

There are no pennies
or favors left, no change.
But might be if we ask for keeps.
There is change.
We must ask for keeps.

           I will come back
           to you for keeps
           after all.
           I will, for your sake,
           for ours.
           The children will rise.

She walks on.
The streets are no longer
desperation.
The reeking vapors
become the quiet wind.
It rains at last.

You can see
how the Chuska Mountains favor
her dreams
when she walks towards them.
Her arms and legs unlimber.
All her love is returning.

The man she finds
is a roadside plant.

She sings then,
the water in her eyes
is clear as a child,
            of rain.
            It shall.
            It shall.
            It shall.
            It shall
            be
            these gifts
            to return
            again.

It will happen again, cleansing.

The People will rise.

For Our Brothers: Blue Jay, Gold Finch, Flicker, Squirrel

Who perished lately in this most unnecessary war, saw them lying off the side of a state road in southwest Colorado

They all loved life.
        And suddenly,
it just stopped for them. Abruptly,
the sudden sound of a speeding
machine,
and that was it.

Blue Jay. Lying there,
his dry eyelids are tiny scabs.
Wartstones, looking ugly.
His legs are just old sticks.
used to push ashes away.
O goddammit, I thought,
just lying there.
Thought of the way he looks,
swooping in a mighty big hurry,
gliding off a fence pole
into a field of tall dry grass,
the summer sunlight catching
a blade of wing, flashing
the bluegreen blackness,
the sun actually black, turning
into the purest flash of light.
And so ugly now, dead.
And nobody knows it except
for those black ants crawling
into and out of decaying entrails.
Nobody but those ants,
and I ask them to do a good job,

128

return Blue Jay completely
back into the earth,
back into the life.

Gold Finch, I took four tiny feathers
from your broken body.
I hope you were looking at me then
out of that life, perhaps
from the nearest hills,
from that young cottonwood tree.
I hope you blessed me.
Until I looked very closely,
I didn't see the fading blood stain
on a wing tip, and I sorrowed for you.
I have always been one to admire
the yellow, the color of corn pollen,
on your tiny feathers as I've seen
you glittering from branch to branch,
whirring and rushing from one tree
to another. I have seen the yellow
of your tiny body and the way
the shades of the cottonwood
and my grandfather's peach trees
could hide you so well
but in a moment your voice
would always speak
and you could be found.
Gold Finch. A pollen bird
with tips of black, flits
his head around and sings
reasonably pretty and revealing.
There you were, forgotten too,
the hard knots of gravel around
and under you, lying besides
the poorly made, cracked asphalt
road upon which sped that hunk
of steel, plastic and chrome.
Well, I'm sorry for the mess.
I'll try to do what I can
to prevent this sort of thing

because, Gold Finch, goddammit,
the same thing is happening to us.

Flicker, my proud brother.
Your ochre wings were meant
for the prayer sticks.
Askew.
Head crushed.
Misshapen.
Mere chips of rottening wood
for your dead eyes.
Crushed.
Askew.
You always were one to fly
too close to flat, open ground.
Crushed.

Squirrel, a gray thing
with bits of brown
where tiny ears joins its head.
Eats seeds, nuts, tender roots,
tiny savory items.
Runs quickly, flashing gray
and sudden.
Throws its head with jerky
nervous motion.
Flicks hardwood shrieks of sound.
Lying by the side of Highway 17,
staring with one dim eye across
the road at underbrush oak,
its body swollen with several days
of death in the hot sun,
its tail a distorted limp twist.
I touch it gently and then try
to lift it, to toss it
into some high grass,
but its fur comes loose.
It is glued heavily
to the ground with its rot
and I put my foot

against it and push it
into the grass, being careful
that it remains upright
and is facing the rainwater
that will wash it downstream.
I smell the waste
of its disintegration
and wipe its fur on my fingers
off with a stone
with a prayer for it
and murmur a curse.

I don't have to ask who killed you.
I know and I am angry and sorry
and wonder what I shall do.

This, for now, is as much as I can do,
knowing your names, telling about you.
Squirrel. Flicker. Gold Finch. Blue Jay.
Our brothers.

"The State's claim that it seeks in no way to deprive Indians
of their rightful share of water, but only to define that
share, falls on deaf ears."

an April 1974 editorial comment
in the Albuquerque Journal

It was beloved old man Clay who used to say:

"It was in 1882, it was they came, and they said that they
would measure up our land. They said it was to assure us of
how much land we owned. It was true that there were those
of us who did not believe that our concern was their purpose,
and we did not want them here. But they did send their men
around our villages and our fields, and they measured how
much land there was, and sometime later—it didn't take them
very long—they told us what their findings came out to be
and that now we could rest assured that the land was recorded
and filed away in their government papers."

The cosmos are measured by American-made satellites,
the land is being razed by Kennecott Copper
and Anaconda Corporation monstrosities,
and our land has been defined by the RIGHT OF WAY
secured by American RAILROADS, ELECTRIC LINES,
GAS LINES, HIGHWAYS, PHONE COMPANIES, CABLE TV.

RAILROADS

My father explained it to me this way,
"When the railroad was first built,
the land was drawn up into townships
and portions of the land were set aside
for schools, grazing, and public utilities.
And then we exchanged some land
with the railroads. They gave us land,

and we gave them some land."
It was only later I figured out that
"they" meant the USA which had given
the railroad the right of way
through our land and also allotted
them land so that what the railroad did
was "give" that land in exchange to us
who were the right of way.

When I was a ten-year-old altar boy,
there were photographs of the railroad
on the church sacristy walls.
They showed 1920 cars and men working
at laying track. There used to be
a watering stop for steam engines
near the church and the American man
who ran the pumps was named McCartys
and that's why the village, Deedzihyama,
I come from is called McCartys
on the official state maps.

ELECTRIC LINES

At first, the electric lines ran
only alongside the railroad tracks
but later they connected up the homes
in Deezihyama and Deechuna with the lines.
Those electric lines connect up Acu
with America.

When they were putting up the lines,
there was this machine.
The machine had a long shiny drill
which it pointed at the ground
and drove it turning into the earth
and almost suddenly there was a hole
in the ground and the machine
drove on to another spot.
A couple of days later, a truck came

133

and threw long black poles
into the holes. At that age,
I didn't know much of anything
and when my young brothers and sisters
asked me what was going on
I probably told them some lies.

GAS LINES

The El Paso Natural Gas pipeline
blew up in the spring of 1966.
Old man Tomato told us what he was doing
on that early morning. He had just gone
out to piss outside his home
and had just come back inside
and was lying on his bed.
"I was singing a hunting song,
and then all of a sudden there was
this strange feeling and then I looked
out the window to the east and saw a light
over the hill beyond Dahska, but I knew
that it wasn't about to be dawn yet."
He told us that at the meeing in Acomita
where the El Paso Natural Gas man said
his company was sorry and they would
send money to make restitution very soon.

The El Paso Natural Gas company ran
through our best garden and left stones.
I was at Indian Boarding School at the time
and so I didn't see it coming through.
It wouldn't have made any difference
whether or not I'd seen it coming through
or whether we'd put a garden in that spring
because it would have come through anyway.
Nobody and nothing could stop it coming through.

HIGHWAYS

In 1952, the Felipe brothers led Nash Garcia
down U.S. 66 unto the reservation
and killed that State cop a few miles east
of Black Mesa. The State panicked
for a couple of months and the brothers
got sent to Federal pen for life.

One night during the Korean War,
my parents and I walked Eagle to the highway.
We stopped at our Aunt Lolita's.
She had made some tamales and she put them
in a paperbag for Eagle to take along.
When we got to the highway,
Eagle showed me how to throw rocks sideways,
skipping them on the pavement to make sparks.
I had never seen that before.
My father flagged the Greyhound with a flashlight
and Eagle went off to Camp Pendleton and Korea.

When the Interstate was coming through,
a place where people had lived a long time ago
was uncovered. I carried one of my nephews—
he was just a kid then—on my back there once.
The old place had four kivas,
and there were many small rooms.
It was built beside a hill to the west
which protected it from the wind.
There was a wash to the east of their home.
When it rains the water flows from the north
unto a wide flat space.
The people planted there, on the south.

PHONE COMPANY

My cousin who was working for a uranium
mill and mine supply company at the time
won some prizes over the telephone.

The voice on the phone from the radio station
asked, "Who is the father of this country?"
He said, "Without thinking about it,
I answered, 'George Washington.' "

I don't think my Grandfather ever used
a telephone in his life although
he did see Eisenhower in Gallup once.
Ike was campaigning for President by train
and that was in the early 1950s.

When I was a boy, I didn't know
whether or not you could talk in Acoma
into the telephone and even after I found
that you could I wasn't convinced
that the translation was coming out correctly
on the other end of the line.
I have to ask the telephone operators
to help. Direct dialing and long distance
information confuse me, and I think
telephone operators are exasperated with me even now.

CABLE TV

As far as I know, no one at Acu
subscribes to cable TV although CATV
from Grants has approached the people
with the idea, saying such things as,
"You can get thirty more channels than you do
presently. You can even get Los Angeles."
What kind of deal is that anyway?
Regular TV is crummy enough. My mother
used to watch "As the World Turns,"
and the kids are getting weird
from being witness to the Brady Bunch.

I don't know much about CATV
and I would like to think
that it's better that way,

but then I get this unwanted feeling
I better learn something about it.

RIGHT OF WAY

The elder people at home do not understand.
It is hard to explain to them.
The questions from their mouths
and on their faces are unanswerable.
You tell them, "The State wants right of way.
It will get right of way."

They ask, "What is right of way?"
You say, "The State wants to go through
your land. The State wants your land."
They ask, "The Americans want my land?"
You say, "Yes, my beloved Grandfather."
They say, "I already gave them some land."
You say, "Yes, Grandmother, that's true.
Now, they want more, to widen their highway."
They ask again and again, "This right of way
that the Americans want, does that mean
they want all our land?"

There is silence.
There is silence.
There is silence because you can't explain,
and you don't want to, and you know
when you use words like industry
and development and corporations
that it wouldn't do any good.

There is silence.
There is silence.
You don't like to think
that the fall into a bottomless despair
is too near and too easy and meaningless.
You don't want that silence to grow
deeper and deeper into you

because that growth inward stunts you,
and that is no way to continue,
and you want to continue.

And so you tell stories.
You tell stories about your People's birth
and their growing.
You tell stories about your children's birth
and their growing.
You tell the stories of their struggles.
You tell that kind of history,
and you pray and be humble.
With strength, it will continue that way.
That is the only way.
That is the only way.

5

I Tell You Now

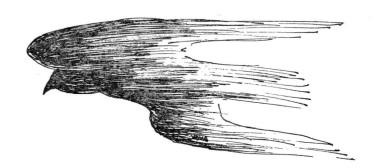

Waking

1.

Woke early this morning,

           old morning moonlight.

Thought of visions,
dreams.
Not the past, not the future,

           just dreams.

Warm life coursing,
flowing through
the circle of everything,
tying me in:

           you're part of it all.
           Don't worry.

Drift back to sleep.

2.

Woke
to a bird fluttering from the sky
through the tipi smokehole.

           Startle

awake
and then smile.

It doesn't happen often.

Back through the smokehole a moment later.
Sent a prayer after it.

Thanks and humility.
All the way into the blue sky.
That is something,
how it happens.
"All the way into the sky."

My Father Singing

My father says,
"This song, I like it
for this one old man."
And my father moves
his shoulders, arms
and hands when he sings
the song.
My father says,
"When the old man
danced this song,
I like it for him."

This Occurs To Me

It has something to do
with intuition and instinct,
a mixture of appreciating
how the physical quality
of dirt and stone exist,
how useful they are,
what you can do with them.
Working with fingers, hands,
the mystery—knowing
it is not a mystery
that you can't possibly
know anything about—
that is yours.
Watching sparrows,
sheer cliff wall,
the effect of light and shadow,
line of stone mesa,
strata of sediment,
touching with foot and hand
the tamp of sand
against cliff wall,
noting the undershadow
of stone ledge.

All these, working in the mind,
the vision of weaving things
inwardly and outwardly
to fit together, weaving stone
together, my father tells me
how walls are built.

Uncle Jose

My sister, Myrna, said,
"Keithy didn't have an Acoma name
so I gave him one.
I called him Hishtiyani,
and I told Uncle Jose."
" 'Histiyani, wah tawa eh
tchishratra,' he said."
Uncle Jose is over ninety.
He knows what good names are.
When he comes to visit, he asks,
"Ehku sthatyumu, Hishtiyani?"
And my sister goes looking
for his brother, Flint Arrowhead.

That time when my sister and I
were leaving our childhood,
Uncle Jose walked us home
late at night from the kiva.
It was very quiet.
When we got to my Auntie's home,
we found apples and oranges
strung together with yucca,
hanging from the door knob.
The next morning was the first day
after the four days had passed,
and we were allowed to eat salt again.

That Time

Agnes' aunt killed the goat.
I held it down, sitting on its belly.
I could feel its whole vibrating life,
the red blood, thinly spurting
in a low arc, and then just flowing.

Brian stood by, his childhands clutched.

Agnes' aunt is a gaunt, thin Navajo woman,
never married, takes care of Chee,
her dead sister's husband.

We skinned the goat, cleaned the guts,
and cut up the meat,
and saved the best parts for Chee.

We put the goat's head in the coals to cook
but the dogs stole it,
and it was half eaten before we found out.

We took the goat meat to a Squaw Dance.
Chee carried it under his arm in a sack,
and he wore his flatbrim hat and a new shirt.

That was that time.

When It Was Taking Place

This morning, the sun has risen
already to the midpoint of where
it will be at the center of the day.
The old man, Amado Quintana,
doesn't get up early anymore.
He still wakes early in the morning
but he can't see the clear things
in the dim light before the sun rises,
and he can't hear the clear sounds.
So he lies on his cot or he sits
in the wooden chair by the stove.
Sometimes he forgets he has not built
the fire in the stove and he wonders
why the weather has changed so early.

He is an old man.
The people in the village
call him Old Man Humped Back.
He has a hump on his back,
and the history about that
is he has lived a long time
and it has grown on him.

This morning at this moment,
Quintana is pointing to the river
below the hill on which he
and his grandson are standing.
He made his grandson help him
climb unto the hill and now
he is showing him the river
and the land before them.
The hill is not very high
and children climb it
to explore and look for things,

but from there you can see
the fields and the canals.

The old man cannot really see
those anymore; his eyes are cloudy
with a gray covering; the only thing
he can see is the sun when it is
at its brightest. Sometimes
he forgets, and he asks why
the weather has changed suddenly
and insists that it must be the times
and the people that are the cause.
But he can see in his mind,
and he tells his grandson,
"You can see that canal that runs
from that gathering of cottonwoods
and then turns to the south
by Faustin's field, that canal
was dug by the first people
who came down from the Old Place.
It was dug then."

He had been a child then,
and he played most of the time,
but he can remember his father
and the others with him.
They dug the canal from the river
to the east and turned to the south,
and then it was easier
as the ground was softer
and the water found its own way.
They had worked and it was good.
They had talked a lot, laughed,
and they got so wearied.
At the end of the day, the men
drug themselves home,
and Amado can remember carrying
his father's handmade shovel
in his hands, and they would be
greeted at their home by his mother.

She would say, "Amo, my partner
and my son, have you worked so hard,"
and she would grab them and hold them
strongly to her.
She would especially make a fuss
over Amado who, at the time,
was their only child.
At that time, they lived in a low
windcarved cave with a wall of stones
along the front of it.

Amado Quintana can see that,
and he points it all out to his grandson,
and he wants him to see all those things,
and he tells the boy, "I was your age then
when it was taking place."

Poems From The Veterans Hospital

8:50 AM Ft. Lyons VAH

The Wisconsin Horse hears the geese.

They wheel from the west.
First the unfamiliar sounds,
and then the memory recalls
ancient songs.

Sky is gray and thick.
Sometimes it is the horizon
and the sky weighs less.

The Wisconsin Horse cranes
his neck.
The geese veer
out of sight
past the edge of a building.

The building is not old,
built in 1937.
Contains men broken
from three American wars.

Less and less, the sound,
and it becomes
the immense sky.

Two Old Men

November 1974

I've seen this old man around. Today as I was walking on
the dike ridge, I saw him at the edge of a marsh looking
for something. I wondered what. Had he lost something?
Was he expecting to find something about yesterday in the
autumn dry weeds and rushes in order that he might insure
tomorrow? I can only speculate. He has never said a word
that I have heard. Surely he speaks or has spoken in his
life but I have never heard.

I've seen you around.
Was it Iowa cornfield edge
or on the outskirts of Minneapolis?
It was late June I think.

Today, I saw you again.
You were moving through a tangle
of autumn rushes taller than you.
You moved so deliberately,
searching every stemmed shadow,
listening to the wind tremble
through the stubble.

You paused at the bottom
of an upslope—
from my distance the marsh
was a dark placid brooding
behind you—
and looked and looked.

What do you search for?
A glint of mica,
a shadow that needs no light,
an echo,
a bit of straw that tastes
of memory?

151

The old man's fingers dance a careful motion that has to
do with knowing the forms and designs that the eyes do not
see, nor even the mind, that mental acknowledgement is only a
part, that in learning a language or a sound, one has to "touch"
the motion of what color it. You have to not only see color
but you must touch it, in a sense become that color, know it,
let it become part of you. I think that old man knows. I
like to watch him. He pushes his steel rim glasses with bony
knuckles back up the bridge of his nose. I call him Touching
Man.

He believes that colors
have shape, texture, substance,
depth, life he can touch.
I know they do.
I believe him.
When he is reaching
his long bony fingers
to a lettered sign
or a dark spot on the sidewalk,
there are the frankest features
of delight, surprise, wonder
in his face.

I believe him.

        Green has cold winter stems
the melted edge of snow
mirrors of angular gravel
see the grain of roots
moving my finger tips

        Chrome rainbows
on fire hydrant curve
meanings
no one sees vividly
by sight or mind
alone touching I see

        Form is not all

nor hearing
for the tensile mass
vibrates against
my tendrils
the mind that sprouts
and reaches into depths
the tips of my fingers

He touches me with the spider tendrils.
I would like to bring him a black rock
from the Lukachukai Mountains and give
it to him without telling him I have
given it to him.

Touching Man, you know things only
a very few know, and that is your strength,
your aloneness.

Damn Hard

Today I remembered
the good buckhorn pocket knife I lost too.

She gave it to me as a surprise one day.
"What's this for?" I asked her.
I'd been drunk a couple of days before
and I wondered why.
"Oh, just because I wanted to," she said.

"I have loved you so damn hard and deeply,"
she wrote in a last letter.

The pocket knife must have cost
thirteen or fourteen dollars
and it felt good and heavy in the hand.

Dammit, I miss that feeling.

153

Today I told Joe, "I still feel crummy.
I almost went and bought one just like it
at a hardware store to replace it but
it wouldn't have been the same thing,
something I lost."

"Yeah, I know," he said.

The other day we were talking,
sitting in front of Building 5.
"I'll never get that screwed up again
about a woman," Kenny said.
A bit later, a woman walked by,
her hips and thighs swinging.
Kenny shook his head and grinned big.
"But you know, it's damn hard not to,"
he said and, knowing, we all laughed.

Yeah, it sure is.

Cherry Pie

We had barbecue beef on buns,
cole slaw with crushed pineapple,
coffee, and cherry pie.
Here in the VAH, at least,
America feeds well the men
it has driven mad.

"My favorite used to be cherry pie."

"Lemon is good too."
"When I was a kid at Indian School,
I worked cleaning yards on weekends.
Walking back to campus at evening,
I'd stop at this cafe on Fourth
and order banana cream pie.
Two slices of pie, boy, that was good."

Deanda hasn't been yelling lately.
They've been feeding him more.
and better mind silencers lately.

Kelly offers his cole slaw.
Nobody wants it, shake their heads.
He offers his bread, we shake our heads.
"He's a dedicated nut," another nut says.

"The only pie I don't like
is mince meat, too rich."

"I wish I was rich."

"I almost married a rich girl once.
She was from Alabama."

There's always something that you almost
did that you should have done.

A cherry pie slips to the floor
off a man's saucer.
He stands there and everything is gone
from his face except sorrow and loss
and it's hard to lose those.

Teeth

After supper, Fuentes tells stories
about his teeth in front of Building 5.
With his gravelly voice, he says,
"Let me tell you guys.

"I used to have partials. Two teeth
and then four teeth. One night I was
with this girl. I put my four teeth
upon the dresser. Early next morning,

still dark, I was looking around
for the bottle, you know, feeling around
on the dresser and all of a sudden
I heard this crunch under my shoe,
you know. It was my teeth, sonofagun.
I said, O what the hell, just teeth.

"Later on, I had another partial.
This time with six teeth. Me and some
other guys were drinking way back
in the hills above El Paso. We were
getting real low and one guy volunteered
to make a run. Fine. He said,
Let me borrow your coat, it's cold.
Sure, I said and gave him my coat.
I had put my teeth in that coat pocket,
sonofagun, and that guy is still on that run."

Travelling

A man has been in the VAH Library all day long,
looking at the maps, the atlas, and the globe,
finding places.
                Acapulco, the Bay of Bengal,
Antartica, Madagascar, Rome, Luxembourg,
places.

He writes their names on a letter pad, hurries
to another source, asks the librarian for a book
but it is out and he looks hurt and then he rushes
back to the globe, turns it a few times and finds
Yokohama and then the Aleutian Islands.

Later on, he studies Cape Cod for a moment,
a faraway glee on his face, in his eyes.
He is Gaugin, he is Coyote, he is who he is,
travelling the known and unknown places,
travelling, travelling.

Superchief

Superchief left on Friday.
I didn't get a chance to see him
before he left but hope he's okay
and stays away from those morning bars
on Central Avenue and Fourth Street.

I saw him one time
up by the Nob Hill Shopping Center.
He had a small paper sack
of oranges and he was sitting
on the curb eating them.
His head was wobbling
from side to side.
He was trying to focus
on the asphalt in front of him.

A white woman watched him
a moment, standing behind him.
She moved on and then halfway
down the block, turned and looked
at him again, shook her head
not in sympathy or pity
but in contempt and disgust.

I tried to remember
his Acoma name as I passed by.
I walked down Silver and my feeling
of being useless was enormous.
I think I even wished my feelings
were as convenient as that woman's.

Even now I can feel
Superchief's withered gray eye
staring at the cement beneath his shoes.

Along The Arkansas River

I walk down to the river.
See four ducks,
two males and two females.
They swim away from me.
I stand very still watching them.

Two fly away then.
I decide to follow downstream.
The water eddys behind
the other two.

I don't follow too close
to the river's edge.
Instead I choose a path
through dry winter willow.

My god I am lonely.
The sand is soft.
I wear tenny shoes.

Around a bend in the river
and upon a stretch of sand bar,
there are many ducks.
They don't seem to see me.
They are not alarmed.
I carry nothing in my hands.
They probably know.

I stand still
and then I slip away
into the winter willow.

Wonder where Coyote is?
Probably in Tulsa by the bridge,
sitting on the grassy bank
near the University, hoping
she's gonna come along

after her three o'clock class
like she said she would.

A freight train was heading south.
Standing in a break of saltcedar
and willow, I got lonesome again.

That's probably where Coyote is.

Looking, Looking

This morning, looking
out the south windows of the Day Room,
I see Ralph standing on the loading dock again.
I call, "Ralph, hey," and he turns to the sound
of my voice two stories high, "Good morning.
What are you doing?"

He says something, points south,
past the dike ridge, the thickets
of spring saltcedar and willows, past
the Arkansas River and the cottonwoods.
He sweeps his hand in a motion
that is an awed gesture: All that land!
All that land! And he turns to me again
and says something and he grins,
pushes his fatigue cap back from his forehead.

"Which way is Taos?" I call.

He points to the southwest then.
Straight over the horizon of low hills.
Further on are the mountains, the mountains.
You just have to climb and then descend
on the other side.
He says things I can't hear, but I know.

"I'll see you later, okay?" I say.

Okay, he nods his head and waves his cap
and looks south again.
He keeps looking south, looking, looking.

For a Taos Man Heading South

Thunder,
the sound from above,
the sound from below,
the sound from everything,
the sound from the rain,
thunder.

I hear thunder as I walk from the Print Shop
to the Canteen.
Thunder from the west and northwest.
The sky is dark with black clouds at the horizon.

The wind is humid and tree branches move slowly.

Rain will be welcome. It's been so long.
"It might rain," someone at Acu will say.
"Yes, it might rain."

Qow kutsdhe neh chah dhyuuh.
Hah uh, qow kutsdhe nehchah dhyuuh.

Let it rain.
Peh eh chah.

Mondragon is going home to Taos today.

"Hey, buddy, good luck now. Okay?
You be good and stay out of those deadly bars.
Okay?"

"Okay yeah," he says.
It will be hard for him but I believe him
when he says, Okay yeah.
I have to. We have to keep believing in ourselves.

Yesterday, a white VA psychologist told us,
"I'm one-eighth Indian but I don't make
a big deal of it," angry at us. "I wish you
weren't going back into the same environment."

Mondragon and I had to tell him, "That's our home,
our land, our people. That's our life. The life
of our people and land and home is who we are."

"You be good and strong now, good buddy.
Come up to Acu. The people are having dances
in July, four days, when the katzina come.
Come visit. Bring your family."

"Okay. I'll come look you up," Mondragon says.

I wave and smile, trying to convey what strength
I have, the significance of my people,
of my belief in him and of myself to him.

Thunder,
the sound from above,
the sound from below,
the sound from everything,
the sound from the rain,
thunder.

Let this be your travelling prayer, Taos brother.
Good things come from below, from above,
from everything, from the rain.
Believe that.
Be strong now, be strong and good with yourself.

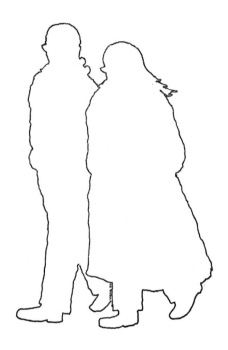

162

I Tell You Now

some things I wanted to tell an
Isleta woman walking by the Gizmo
store, 2nd & Central, Albuquerque

I really have no words to match your stride.
You have two young children with you,
and they are probably your grandchildren.
I like the red flowered shawl over your head
and the starched lace on your wrists.
The Gizmo store, the yellowpaint walls,
plate window glass, and For Sale signs,
the cement pavement under your wornheel shoes—
all look out of place, even Albuquerque.

As I said, I really have no words which are equal.
Even the sheaf of written stories
I am carrying under my arm to the printers
because as I watch you, the stories
which I did work carefully at lack the depth
and the meaning of your walk.
O I guess the words are adequate enough—
they point out American depredations,
the stealing of our land and language,
how our children linger hungry and hurt
on streetcorners like the ones I just passed,
but then I get the feeling that these
words of my youth are mere diatribes.
They remain useless and flat when what I really wish
is to listen to you and then have you listen to me.
I've been wanting to tell you for a long time.

I tell you now.

A short time before my wife gave birth to our son, I
went down to your Pueblo to write a story for a newspaper
for thirty dollars which we needed. I talked with an older
man. He was cleaning a horse corral. I asked him about

163

the huge tree by the railroad crossing. He said, "I don't
know how old it is. It's been there as long as I can remember."
He invited me to the San Augustine Fiesta the coming week-
end. The story I wrote was about the tree and the older man.

I like the story about the people handcuffing the
Catholic priest, leading him to the edge of the village,
and telling him never to come back. You know, the one with
the German name who told you, the people, you were pagan
and even had the earth of your church cemented over.

I like telling people that Isleta has the hottest chili
along the Rio Grande.

Sometime ago, an American poet friend and I watched the
people dancing in the plaza. He remarked, "Nowhere else in
America can you see something like this." There were over a
hundred dancers, young and old, and others were singing.

A longtime friend lives by the church. He's been around.
Almost became a lawyer once, worked in Maine, Florida, even
for the Indian affairs of the USA. Even was a hippie for a
while, did a lot of dope, acted crazy and worried people, but
I hope he's okay now.

The fight the Isleta people put up against the State when
the State wanted to use your land for an Interstate was really
something. The people turned the money down, told the State
to go to hell, and the State got all pissed and frustrated.
That was really something.

Once on the way home from the Army, I met an Isleta girl
in Albuquerque and we spent two days in town before I
thought I had better go home.

In El Paso, almost ten years ago, I met a man and woman
and their three children. The man said they had relatives up
north on the river and said some day they were going to visit
because it had been a long time since they had come south.

One of the stories that's sort of funny but I don't like
is about the pickle packing plant that failed and the building
is setting empty and useless now because the American
government never meant for it to succeed.

I don't like the fact that one Fall a family was killed
by a train at the crossing into the village because the
AT&SFRY railroad never bothered to protect you when they
laid their tracks through your land.

These few things then,
I am telling you
because I do want you to know
and in that way
have you come to know me now.

Printed in October 1977 in Santa Barbara
for Turtle Island Foundation by Mackintosh & Young.
Design by Graham Mackintosh.
Two thousand copies were printed in
ten point Trump Mediaeval,
of which one hundred were hand-bound in boards.
Twenty-six copies were numbered and signed
by the author.